# A MIST OF MEMORIES

# A MIST OF MEMORIES

## KATE BLAIR

We acknowledge financial support for our publishing activities: the Government of Canada, through the Canada Book Fund and The Canada Council for the Arts; the Government of Ontario, through the Ontario Arts Council, Ontario Creates, and the Ontario Book Publishing Tax Credit. We acknowledge additional funding provided by the Government of Ontario and the Ontario Arts Council to address the adverse effects of the novel coronavirus pandemic.

Library and Archives Canada Cataloguing in Publication

Title: A mist of memories / Kate Blair.
Names: Blair, Kate, author.
Identifiers: Canadiana (print) 20230169392 | Canadiana (ebook) 20230169406 |
ISBN 9781770866966 (softcover) | ISBN 9781770866973 (HTML)
Classification: LCC PS8603.L3153 M57 2023 | DDC jC813/.6—dc23

United States Library of Congress Control Number: 2023932190

Cover art: Emily Weedon
Author photograph: Calvin Thomas
Interior text design: Marijke Friesen
Manufactured by Friesens in Altona, Manitoba in March, 2023.

**MIX**
Paper from
responsible sources
FSC
www.fsc.org
**FSC® C016245**

Printed using paper from a responsible and sustainable resource, including a mix of virgin fibres and recycled materials.

Printed and bound in Canada.

DCB Young Readers
An imprint of Cormorant Books Inc.
260 Ishpadinaa (Spadina) Avenue, Suite 502, Tkaronto (Toronto), ON  M5T 2E4
www.dcbyoungreaders.com
www.cormorantbooks.com

To everyone who kept things going during the pandemic,
in any way they could.

And to my dad, who can beat this cancer.

# PART ONE

# CHAPTER ONE

## OLEANDER

Mist seethes in the dark of the underground temple. A tendril creeps forward and an image forms within, separating from the blackness of the fog: a lost memory, tight and dark.

The moment unspools until it is finally clear; a scene hanging upon the air like a projection; a memory of a borrowed boat on dark water.

A girl sits in it as it drifts. There has been no wind to fill the sail for hours. She checks her phone: still no reception. Her jean shorts leave her legs exposed to the evening chill and the damp of the fog. The wind tosses her purple hair as she stares ahead shivering, eyes wide. She flinches away from the edge of the boat, from the images in the mist that surrounds her.

She knows she has made a terrible mistake.

The waves slap lightly against the fiberglass hull as the haze thins a little, and she finally has a break from the visions that have tormented her for hours.

Out of the fog lurches the land she has been looking for. The bare spike of bushes crowns the crumbling cliffs, and she cries out with relief.

Her triumph is short-lived. Rocks black as burned bone, sharp as teeth, rip out of the waves ahead of her. She pulls on ropes, tightening the sails, hoping for a miracle. When it doesn't come, she sticks her arm in the chill of the water and paddles desperately.

She is no match for the tide. The relentless waves carry her ship into the stones.

After the crash, she bails with her hands, but her fingers cannot hold back the sea. She did not steal a life jacket, and when her boat sinks, the undercurrent grabs at her kicking legs. The shore is not far, but she is cold and weak. As she struggles, as the spiteful waves slap her and one purple shoe slips off her thrashing feet, she thinks of everything she left behind, everything that she will never escape: her father's suicide; Rupert, the photograph, and the weight of regret.

As the cold water leeches the last of the strength from her, she wonders if it would be better this way. She wanted to be forgotten. She wanted to leave it all behind. On some level, wasn't this what she was looking for when she started searching for the island?

Finally, inevitably, her cares and her clothes drag her down.

The water closes over her head.

# CHAPTER TWO

## AJAY

MISSING.

It was still a gut-punch to see the word printed across the top of the poster.

*Oleander Dillon, 17 years old, 5'5".*

She grinned at me from the soggy paper stapled to the skeletal tree.

*Last seen July 20 at around 3 p.m. on Southcliff Pier. Purple ombré hair. Wearing a gray shirt, jean shorts, and purple Converse trainers.*

It was October. I'd last seen Oleander on one of the hottest days of the year, and now the gutters were full of rotting leaves. She wasn't coming back; I had to face it. I swallowed and tried to hold it together.

The wet paper had ripped away from the trunk at one corner and flapped in the cold wind. I tried to push it back, to attach it to the tree properly, so other passersby could see her, would know to look for her, but the page was too damp. My thumb went right through it.

I stared at the hole I'd made.

I'd destroyed her face. Changed her into just another missing girl.

"What are you doing?" The voice was outraged.

A woman clutched paper against her chest, a staple gun in her hand. Her long brown hair was frizzy, and her furrowed brow and the set of her jaw was familiar. She was looking past me, at the poster.

"I didn't mean to. It kind of ripped."

I felt like crap saying it. It sounded like a pathetic excuse.

Her eyes flicked to me. "Ajay, right?"

That was one of the things about being brown in a mostly white small town; you were never anonymous. Well, it was probably that and the fact I still wore a face mask everywhere. I wondered what Oleander had said about me. If she'd spoken about me at all.

"You're Oleander's mum, right?"

She nodded, still staring at the picture I'd destroyed.

"Sorry."

She turned her attention to me. The wind blew her thick scarf and rustled the papers in her hands.

"Well," she said, finally. "If you really want to fix it, you can help me." She shoved the papers into my hands, then took one from the top of the pile. They were copies of the same poster, but these were dry and new. She peeled the wet version off the tree and stapled the new poster up.

A thought struck me. "You do this every time it rains?"

"I only just started putting these up. I've given up on the police. They've barely looked. But I'll need to get these laminated next time." She took a deep breath. "If I can afford it. Come on, then."

We moved on to the next tree.

It took over an hour to replace all the posters. We trudged through the wet leaves, talking about Oleander between the clack of the staple gun. I held the paper flat against trees and poles for her. By the time we'd put up fifty or so, she'd relaxed a little. She even insisted on me calling her Sarah, which was good, because "Ms. Dillon" felt weird, like she was a teacher.

"I heard you lost a sister," she said.

I nodded. I wondered if she'd heard from small-town gossip or if Oleander had told her that it was my fault Meera died.

"Sorry about that. But you have some idea what it's like, right? To lose someone you love."

"Yeah." My voice went a bit weird.

"Did Oleander tell you where she was going?"

I shook my head. "Sorry."

"I didn't even know that was going on, with her and that Rupert guy, and the photo. Did she discuss any of that with you?"

"She wasn't really talking to me by the time she left." It hurt to say it.

"But you used to be friends. You knew her from school, right?"

"We were in the same year, but we met at the gift shop."

"I didn't know that."

"She's one of the first people I met in Southcliff. She helped me get a job."

"You worked at the Treasure Chest too?" Sarah said.

"Next door."

"You know she quit just before she disappeared?"

"Yeah."

"That's one of the reasons the police think she ran away." Sarah narrowed her eyes, evaluating me. "She had printed out photos up in her bedroom, with Post-its stuck on them. I think she might have been deciding where to go. Would you mind looking at them? Maybe you can help me work it out."

I didn't hesitate. "Of course."

Oleander Dillon's house was a small modern semi, on a road of identical small modern semis in orangey brick, squeezed together with only an alleyway to the back yards between each pair. A climbing vine had been planted at the front of hers. It had been pretty in late spring, covered with pink flowers when I'd walked her home from work a couple of times. Now it was brown and soggy with October rain.

I took my shoes off at the door automatically, but Sarah didn't. I wasn't sure whether to put mine back on again, but that seemed rude, so I followed her in my socked feet, feeling awkward.

The house was smaller than mine, but they had about twice as much stuff as we did. The hall was lined with cupboards and shelves. There was barely room for all the furniture in the living room, and the coffee table was covered with photo albums. Pictures of Oleander as a baby and a little girl were scattered over the sofa and chairs.

"I'm sorry the place is such a mess," Sarah said.

"It's fine. It's nice."

The stairs went directly up from the back of the living room, and she led me that way. As we went along the narrow upstairs hall, I noticed they had carpets everywhere, even the bathroom. I tried to think of something to say, something normal, but Oleander's mum stared ahead at the shut door at the end of the hall. She took a deep breath.

"I haven't changed anything. I kept it just as she left it, except the note."

"The note?"

"It just said she had to go, and to forget about her." Her mother gave a dry laugh. "As if I could."

She opened the door, and we stepped in.

The first thing I noticed were the Post-its. The yellow of the paper stuck out, scattered over photos tacked to one of the walls. As I got closer I could see the pictures under the Post-its were normal photos, pictures of friends and family, printed in color on paper. Oleander posed in selfies with Tisha and others on school trips and holidays. There were ones of Sarah and Oleander at various ages, as well as a few with her dad.

"I come in here a lot," Sarah said. "I just like to see her."

I nodded, caught up in the images. The Post-its on them had place names in Oleander's handwriting, showing where they'd been taken: London, Bristol, Plymouth, Exeter, and one that caught my eye. It was of Oleander and her dad, in front of a sign. The island's name was written on a Post-it too, something French-sounding.

I'd seen this picture before. The last time I'd seen Oleander.

"Where's this?" I said, reading out the name.

Oleander's mother peered at it. Then she shrugged. "Never heard of it."

Funny, how it had slipped from my mind, until I saw the picture again.

"She showed me this picture," I said.

"When was that?"

"July. She showed me the same photo of this island during that big heat wave in July."

Sarah tilted her head. Her expression was just as unreadable as her daughter's.

"Sorry, what island?"

I shook my head. I still couldn't remember the stupid name. I looked back at the Post-it. The name was obvious when I read it again. It was daft that I'd forgotten. I turned back to Sarah, but the word slipped from my mind again.

I was thinking I was a complete bloody idiot, when I remembered Oleander laughing, back when she'd shown me the picture, as if me forgetting it was the point.

Maybe it was.

I looked back at the place name. Another, earlier memory came back to me: Oleander with a green book at the gift shop. The island's name was in the title of that, too. "I think she was reading about that island too."

"Where's the island?"

"Nearby, Oleander said."

Oleander's mother shrugged, and I wondered if she'd forgotten about the island again, just like I had.

"She can't be anywhere nearby, someone would have seen her by now. She's probably gone somewhere she wouldn't be found easily, like a city."

"Can I use a pen?" I asked.

Sarah nodded, looking confused.

I grabbed the nearest one from Oleander's desk, rolled up my sleeve, and copied the words from the Post-it onto my arm, in bright blue ink.

LEVAY ISLAND.

Sarah pointed at the place names on the Post-its. "But perhaps she was deciding where to run to. She'd have needed help, someone who knew the city she was going to." She gave me a sharp look. "You said you're new to Southcliff, right?"

I nodded, suddenly not liking where this was going. "New-ish."

"Where did you say you were from?"

"London."

She put her finger on the Post-it that said "London." It was a picture of Oleander in front of Tower Bridge.

"Did you take this?"

"No."

"Where is she?"

"I don't know."

"Please, just tell me."

"I don't know! I really don't!"

Tears were forming in her eyes. She took hold of my hand. "It's okay if you helped her run away. I know she was going through a lot. Is that why you destroyed her picture? You wanted to keep her hidden?"

"That was an accident. I'm not hiding her, I swear."

She gave a breathless gasp. "I just want to know if she's okay. Can you ask her to call, please? It's been three months. I ... I can't eat. I can't sleep. I don't know what to do. Please."

I pulled out of her grip, gently. She looked like a drowning woman, reaching to me for help. "You must know where she is. Someone must."

"I'd tell you if I did. I really would. I promise."

Her mouth kept moving, shaping the word *please*.

I backed away. "I should go. Sorry."

She didn't try to stop me. She just watched until I was out of sight along the landing.

I walked down the stairs as normally as I could manage, put my shoes on and ran off down the street.

# CHAPTER THREE

## OLEANDER

The office is plain, decorated in tasteful grays. Oleander sits in a gray armchair, used tissues damp and crumpled in her hand. She wants to stuff them in her mouth, right down her throat, to try to smother the scream that threatens to come out.

Next to her is her mother. They face a simple desk, a middle-aged man sitting behind it. He has a slim file closed in front of him, along with a desk phone, a box of tissues, and a brass nameplate identifying him as Gerald Buxton.

"He does not appear to have updated his will since your divorce was finalized, but I'm afraid he had very little in the way of assets."

Oleander's mother shakes her head. "That can't be right."

"I can only speak to the information I have here, but once his liabilities —"

"He was paid a ton. He had that big house and the classic car. He'd just come back from Thailand."

"Please, Mum, don't."

"I want to make sure you get what you should. He must have money hidden away. He did that when they were working out the child support."

"Your ex-husband's house was rented and it appears his car and his recent holiday had been paid for with loans. Perhaps his lifestyle expenditures are why he left so few assets?"

Sarah's jaw tightens. "This is so like him, to leave us screwed again. I can't take on any more shifts at the home. I barely see my daughter as it is."

Oleander reaches for the tissue box again, but it's empty.

The solicitor presses a button on his phone. "Rupert, can you bring some more tissues?"

"Even apart from the mortgage, how am I meant to afford university for her now?"

"I'm sorry I don't have better news for you, Ms. Dillon. I know this is a very difficult time for your family."

"That selfish —"

"Mum!"

Gerald Buxton steeples his fingers. "Maybe your daughter could use a break from this."

Oleander shakes her head quickly. "I'm okay," she lies.

The door to the office opens then, and in steps a young man, carrying tissues. He's tall with a neatly cut mop of blond hair and bright gray eyes. He puts the tissues on the table and turns to leave.

"Rupert, could you take the young lady out for a moment? Perhaps make her a cup of tea?"

For a moment, Rupert looks annoyed, but his gaze falls on Oleander, and his expression softens into a smile. "Of course."

"I'm really fine."

"I'll tell you about anything you miss," her mother says.

"It's just paperwork," the solicitor adds.

Oleander knows she's outnumbered. She wants to argue, but they're just going to clam up until she's gone anyway.

Rupert shows her into an almost-identical office, although the name plate on this desk reads "Sharon Chen." "Sharon's on her hols, so we won't be disturbed." He closes the door gently behind them, and gestures to an empty chair. Oleander sinks into it. Rupert sits next to her.

Oleander rubs at her tears with her hands, wishing her dress had sleeves. She tries to wipe her palms on the fabric of the chair, subtly.

"Sorry, I should have brought the tissues."

"It's okay." She takes a deep breath and looks at him properly.

He's good-looking, she realizes. Very good looking. She'd been too preoccupied in the other room to notice, but now they're alone, and he's sitting so close to her, she finds she has to try not to stare at those bright gray eyes, and his perfectly square jaw.

He's wearing a well-fitting suit with a white shirt underneath. She can smell him too, not the overwhelming stench of body spray her male classmates seem to favor, but a citrusy, subtle smell.

He's leaning toward her, elbows on his thighs, hands clasped. His fingers are inches from her tight-clad knees.

Oleander swallows and looks down at her hands. "Sorry."

"You're upset. It's only natural. You've just lost your father."

She swallows down the guilt. She didn't "lose" him. She abandoned him.

"You seem a bit young to be a solicitor," she says.

Rupert looks awkward. "Just qualified."

"That's cool." Oleander feels stupid as soon as she's said it. She wonders how old he is. Twenty-one, perhaps? Older? Can you be a solicitor straight out of uni?

"Do you want to talk?"

She shrugs.

"I don't know what was happening in there, but you were star-ing daggers at your mother."

"That's normal though, right? Like, no one gets on with their mums. It's a fact."

"You must be going through a very difficult time."

She feels exposed. "You know … about us?"

"I don't mean to pry, and you don't have to say anything. But yes, I do know a little about your family from what's on file."

She feels nauseous. There wouldn't be anything on the file on her part in her dad's death, would there? She can't imagine how there could be. She examines his expression and there's nothing but sympathy in his wide gray eyes. She relaxes, slightly.

"So … you know my dad killed himself."

He nodded. "But it's clearly your mother you're angry at."

"I'm not really angry at her. I just … she's been mad at him since the divorce, you know? But now he can't even defend himself."

"That must be hard."

"I'm not expecting her to be heartbroken or anything, but it makes it impossible to talk to her about this."

"You need someone to talk to. Someone who understands."

"We can barely cover the bills. We can't afford a therapist."

"Look …" Rupert reaches into his pocket. "I shouldn't do this. But here."

He hands over a business card.

"Message me if you want to talk. I'm not a therapist, but I'm a good listener, I promise."

Oleander takes the card, and as she does so, he cups her hand in his, warm and intimate. Her breathing catches.

"No pressure. Feel free to chuck this in a bin. Just … don't tell your mother, or my boss, okay? I shouldn't offer, but …"

Before Oleander can say anything, there's a knock on the door. Rupert lets go of her, and stands, stepping back. Oleander closes her fist around the card and slips her hand into her lap.

Oleander's mother opens the door. "All done, although it was barely worth coming. Let's go home." She looks at her daughter's tear-streaked face. "I'm really sorry, sweetie. Look, I've got a bit of time before the night shift. I'll make tacos. How about that?"

As Oleander stands, she glances back at Rupert. He's standing with his hands behind his back, looking professional. If she couldn't feel the edges of his card cutting into the palm of her hand, she'd think she'd imagined the whole thing.

Oleander types several messages to Rupert but deletes each of them.

Was she misreading things or was there a vibe back there? He's cute. Like ridiculously cute. She didn't know they made faces that perfect in real life. But he was probably just being kind, offering a sympathetic ear to a troubled teen.

She does want someone to talk to, someone better at listening than her mother, or Tisha, who is an awesome best friend in most ways, but has no idea how to handle the new, sad Oleander.

Is it really such a huge stretch that there might have been something between them? She's been mistaken for a uni student before. She's nearly seventeen. There's only four years between them, if he's twenty-one.

Finally, Oleander writes the simplest message she can think of, and hits "send" before she can change her mind. Immediately, she feels stupid. He was being polite, that's all. She's just bothering him.

But the reply pops up almost immediately.

*I'm so glad you messaged. I'd been hoping you would.*

She waits for him near a park on the edge of town, like he asked. She's early and it's colder than she thought. She wishes she hadn't worn a short skirt. She paces to keep warm, looking at the pictures of her dad that she's uploaded to her phone.

There are pictures of her tiny hand in his, in front of a castle when she was a toddler; three grinning faces from when her family was still young and whole. There are toes stuck in the sand of a French beach a year later, still the three of them, her father's nose red with sunburn. Then later photos, selfies she took of the every-other-weekend visits she used to have with him: trips to theme parks and museums before those became few and far between. He blamed the pandemic for keeping them apart after the divorce, but it started before then, and as things got back to normal he had other excuses: he was too busy; he was too tired.

Then his girlfriend left him and the real problems began.

At first Oleander was happy that he was back in touch. There's a selfie on her phone she took of the two of them in his favorite pub, where he let her have beer or wine. He needed someone to talk to about his break-up. At the beginning she was proud that he thought she was worthy of trust. She didn't mind answering when her phone woke her in the middle of the night. She was happy he thought she was such a good listener.

But it soon became clear that she wasn't helping. He got worse, turned bitter. She didn't like the way he talked about Fiona, the misogynistic language he used. She suspected he was drunk when he contacted her; his messages were full of badly spelled words and weird autocorrects.

When she suggested he might need professional help he took it personally. He accused her of trying to palm him off onto leeches who would charge him hundreds of pounds to make him whine about his mother or put him on drugs to zombify him.

Soon, she found she was the one with excuses, but he kept messaging.

Once, he showed up at her house with beery breath, on a night he knew her mum was working. He asked if they could go somewhere so he could talk, but she didn't want to get in a car with him when he'd been drinking. She lied and said she had a friend coming over.

She wasn't sure if she should let him drive home, but he insisted he'd only had the one beer and wouldn't let her call a taxi. She didn't know how to stop him, short of getting him arrested. She watched him pull out of her road and messaged twenty minutes later to make sure he got home safe.

In the pictures on Oleander's phone, her father sometimes grins, but as time passes his expression is more and more strained.

She wonders why she never noticed that, until it was too late.

Rupert pulls up, leans over the passenger seat and opens the door from inside.

"I'm so sorry I asked you to meet out here. I didn't know it would be so cold," he says. "Get in, and I'll crank up the heat to warm you up."

Oleander climbs in, while Rupert leans over to the back seat, picks up a bouquet and hands it to her: a dozen white roses.

"Thank you." She clutches them, a little startled from the gesture.

"White roses are for friendship," he says.

"Friendship. Nice." She hopes she's hidden the disappointment in her voice. Of course she's too young for him. She was silly to think he could be interested. Still, she appreciates the gesture. It's nice to know where she stands before she embarrasses herself.

He pulls away from the curb and she struggles to strap herself in while holding the flowers. "I'm sorry I was such a mess in your office."

He waves a hand. "Will readings are always emotional. It happens at a job like mine. You obviously needed someone to talk to."

"Thanks so much for offering," she says.

"It's my pleasure. Honestly, I appreciate the excuse to get out of the house."

Oleander nods. "Your parents driving you up the wall, too?"

He grins, as if what she's said is adorable. "I don't live with my parents. But my housemate has been, yes."

Oleander looks out of the side window to cover her embarrassment. "He's annoying you then?"

"She is. But we're not here to talk about my problems. I wanted to see how you were holding up."

"I'm okay."

"How are things with your mother?"

She shrugs. "Not great. She's trying, though."

"But ...?"

"She's worried about money. About paying for my university. She works a lot. That's why she was like that at your office. Sorry."

"She's a nurse, right?"

"She works at a nursing home. She's a care assistant."

"Well, you seem smart. Maybe you can get a scholarship of some kind. Or support yourself with modeling."

Oleander looks sharply at him, to see if he's joking. But he's staring at the road, and his gaze hasn't flickered. She knows she's not hideous or anything, but she's definitely not model material.

"I'm sorry. I'm getting off track. You were talking about your mother."

The compliment was too big, too unexpected. She's not sure how to respond. She looks down at the white flowers, wrapped in crinkly plastic that sticks to her hands. He was complimenting her as a friend, obviously.

"I … She's impossible to talk to. My best friend isn't much better. She just keeps saying I'm feeling guilty for no reason."

He glances at her. "Feeling guilty? What for?"

She wants to kick herself. She didn't mean to get into that. But he threw her off with the ridiculous modeling comment.

"Um. Where is it we're going?"

"You're going to love it. We're not far now."

But it's another fifteen minutes before they arrive. The restaurant is two towns over. It's clearly expensive, and Oleander feels out of place as they step into the elegant, dimly lit room. It looks romantic. If it weren't for him making things clear with the flowers, she'd think this was a date.

Red tablecloths drip from intimate tables. Dark velvet wallpaper congeals in the corners behind the candlelight. The murmur of polite conversation and the genteel tinkle of cutlery fill the air as a man in a suit leads Rupert and Oleander to their table.

Oleander takes it all in, wide-eyed. It's easily the nicest restaurant she's been to. Rupert pulls a chair out for her, and she sits awkwardly, tugging her black skirt down over her bare legs.

Rupert takes his own seat and smiles over the table. "I hope you don't mind me bringing you all the way here. I wanted to take you somewhere quiet so you could relax and talk, somewhere we won't be interrupted by anyone we know."

"It's lovely." She opens the menu and bites at the inside of her cheek as she reads the prices.

"Obviously, the meal is my treat," Rupert says.

"Thank you, that's very generous." Oleander still frowns at the list. She doesn't want to order anything too expensive and seem greedy, but the menu is in French, and she doesn't know what half the dishes are.

Rupert seems to notice her awkwardness. "I can order for you if you want. I know this place well."

She exhales, glad he's so thoughtful. "That's probably a good idea. Thanks." She closes her menu and looks around at the room as the waiter returns and takes Rupert's order.

They are the youngest people there, by some margin, and she notices the eyes on them, watching almost hungrily. Rupert draws the gaze of the room. He exudes old-fashioned charm, matching the restaurant perfectly.

She pulls down her skirt again.

"Relax. You look lovely."

"Thanks." She pushes her hair behind her ears, but it quickly escapes again, falling back over her cheek.

"No, I mean it. You have a black-and-white film star look about you. I mean, if you didn't have the purple hair. If you cut it short, you'd be the spitting image of a twenties movie star, like Clara Bow."

She nods. Her fingers itch to grab her phone so she can google the name.

The waiter brings a bottle of wine to the table and makes a show of displaying it to them on a white cloth. He pours a little for Rupert, who sips it, and nods. The waiter fills both their glasses.

Oleander looks at the red wine in front of her nervously. "So. I really don't know anything about you. How … old are you?"

"Early twenties. You're basically seventeen, right?"

"Yes. You know that from our file?"

He nods at her glass of wine and winks. "I won't tell the waiter if you won't."

Oleander's shoulders relax slightly. She picks up her glass and takes what she hopes is a sophisticated-looking sip. She's not sure what to do with her hands, so finds herself taking a few more sips. She's relieved when the waiter returns, carrying two plates with elegantly balanced towers of small white disks.

"Sautéed scallops," Rupert says. Oleander watches carefully to see which fork he picks up and mirrors him as he takes his first bites. He smiles, encouragingly. It does taste good, mostly of garlic and butter. There's not much of it, and Rupert is done with his quickly.

"So," he says, putting his cutlery down. "How are you doing?"

She struggles to swallow her mouthful quickly so she can reply. "Good. Well, I mean no. Not good. But you know."

"How are things with your mother?"

Oleander shakes her head. "She doesn't really get it. She can't ever see my father as anyone other than the man she divorced."

"Divorce is so sad. That must have been hard for you."

"It's better that they're divorced. Trust me. But they were happy once. I made a photo album. I've got some pictures from back when they were together." She reaches for her phone, then stops herself, looking around. "But this doesn't seem like the kind of place I should be on my phone."

Rupert gives a little laugh. "Maybe not. But perhaps you could show me later?"

Oleander quickly turns off the screen and puts it face down on the table. She takes another sip of her wine.

"Sorry."

"You have nothing to be sorry for," Rupert says, gently. "But you were talking about your mother."

"Oh, yes. I mean, she's upset at him for killing himself, and for leaving us with nothing, not even the child support money, and I guess that's kind of understandable, but it's hard."

A waiter appears, removing their plates smoothly.

"Your parents divorced, and your mother resented your father. Do you think that had something to do with … what he did?"

Oleander takes a gulp of wine and finds her glass is empty.

The waiter is at her elbow almost immediately, refilling her glass.

"Slowly, okay?" Rupert whispers as the waiter departs.

"No," Oleander says.

"What?"

"Sorry. I didn't mean 'no' about the wine. I meant about Mum. I don't think that's why he did it."

"Why do you think he did it?"

She can feel the memory like a dark shape underwater, threatening to surface. She can't let it. Not here, not now. She can't tell him. She's not even sure she could get the words out. And if he knew the truth, he'd hate her.

She picks up her glass, gulps down the wine.

"I … don't know. But I should have listened to him more. Been there for him more."

"I'm sure you did all you could. I heard you were the one who found him."

Another nod. Another swig of wine.

He swears under his breath. "Wow. I'm so sorry. That's … you shouldn't have had to go through that. No one should."

She's clutching her wine glass so hard she's surprised it doesn't shatter.

She tries to breathe, tries not to panic, tries to focus on the flicker of the candle on the table between them. She tries to push down the images that threaten the fragile grip she has on herself, tries to keep it submerged.

She looks back up at Rupert and plasters a smile on her face.

"That's enough about me. Let's talk about you. What made you decide to be a solicitor?"

The question feels inane to her, but Rupert brightens.

"It's a funny story, actually."

It turns out to be a long story, and she's grateful for that. She wonders if he could see she was struggling and he's trying to take her mind off things. And he's right, it is funny. It's about a prank gone wrong, where Rupert stopped a pub landlord from calling the police on his friends by pretending to be a lawyer. She laughs in all the right places, but when she tries to talk, her tongue stumbles over the words, like stones in her mouth. She's drunk too much.

She eats when her coq au vin comes, although she can barely taste it. The bones are awkward, and she's uncoordinated with the wine. She doesn't want to make a mess, so she ends up leaving most of the meat on the thing.

Rupert doesn't ask any more questions and she's relieved, even though she's not sure if she's bored him, or if he's being considerate. It's nice not to talk, nice to stare at his handsome face, nice to have something else to think about. This restaurant, this man, this wine make her feel like someone else, no longer Oleander Dillon, and she likes it.

She struggles to stay awake on the drive home, digging her nails into her palms as the alcohol tightens its grip. She should have listened to him, should have drunk slower. Rupert opens the car door for her back at the park where he picked her up, and she stumbles out.

"I'm so glad you opened up to me."

She doesn't feel open. She feels clenched tight, a ball wrapped around the memory that she can't face.

But it has been a good night, or at least better than the nights she's become used to, crying alone in her bedroom. It's the wine making her feel nauseous tonight, not the shame. The evening has been a distraction. The booze has numbed the sharp edges of her grief.

Rupert looks thoughtful. "You know, I thought I was doing you a favor, taking you out so I could lend an ear. But I had a great time with you tonight. You're much more mature than I expected. You're interesting, and a really good listener."

"Thanks."

He looks awkward. "Would you like to go out again sometime? Not just for someone to talk to, but maybe, you know …"

It's the wine that makes her blurt out the word. "A date?"

He gives a rueful laugh. "I guess so. If it's not totally out of line for me to ask. We can absolutely just stay friends if you would prefer. But it might be nice. What do you think?"

Dizzy in the gray of his gaze, Oleander nods.

# CHAPTER FOUR

## AJAY

I'd first met Oleander back in March.

Pa and Amma had insisted on me getting a weekend job, because they were big on me getting "real work experience." In London, where I'd worked at my cousin's hair salon, I'd asked how sweeping up hair and making tea was meant to help me get anything other than a dead-end job.

"You never know what might help. Remember Vihaan? Lots of people who went for his job at the auction house had masters' degrees too, but they had all those big sculptures, and he was the only one —"

"With experience driving a forklift. Yes, Pa, I know."

There was never any point in arguing with them, even when Pa told me to job hunt the old-fashioned way, dropping off paper resumes. I tried explaining that everyone looked online. He said that was the best reason for doing it in person.

"If everyone else is online, you'll beat them to it!"

That's why I was working my way along the row of tourist traps that littered the Southcliff seafront on a warm March afternoon.

My mate Jal had teased me endlessly about moving to the seaside, so when I'd spotted the gift shop, with unicorn floaties hanging outside, I knew I had to go in.

A bell tinkled as I entered. At the end of a narrow aisle, the girl at the counter looked up. She had curly purple hair, falling past her shoulders. She gave me a quick smile, then turned back to her phone.

She was pretty, but obviously preoccupied. I focused on the aisles, looking for something that might make Jal laugh. They had a big rack of seaside rocks with names in them, but the J section wasn't going to have "Jalpesh" so I moved to the next shelf.

I found my gaze being drawn back to the purple-haired girl. She caught me looking at her, and smiled again. A cheekier smile this time. I liked it.

I kept browsing, checking out cheap shell jewellery and jars of layered, colored sand.

This time, when I glanced back at her, she was already grinning, as if she'd been expecting me to look again.

"Is there something in particular you're looking for? Novelty pencil? Cuddly squid?"

"Hi. Um … I want something tacky."

She put a hand on her chest, mock offended. "We do not sell tack here. Only quality gifts to make magical memories. Can I interest you in one of our finest rude T-shirts? Or perhaps sir would care to peruse our exquisite selection of shell sculptures, each complete with googly eyes and seaside pun-based catchphrases?"

I wondered if she could tell how wide I was grinning behind my mask. I liked her big hazel eyes and the way her face lit up as she teased me.

"The shell sculptures sound awesome. Where are those?"

"Over there." She gestured to the shelves on the left side. I crouched down. They were glued-together little creatures, each made of small shells and pebbles, mounted on a larger clam, with a few words painted across the bottom. I read the first: *Keep Clam and Carry On.*

"Perfect." I could imagine Jal's expression.

"Are you really going to get one? Why?"

"Just moved here from London. Want to send something back to my mate. Something seaside-y."

"Well then, you could pick 'I Shell Miss You' or if you're in the mood for something more motivational, I'd recommend 'Seas the Day,' which is my personal favorite, as you can tell by the fact that I'm living the dream of working retail in a seaside gift shop."

I leaned forward. "'Seas the Day' is cool. Oh no, wait. This one."

Googly eyes had been stuck on a white cowrie shell, with a pointed brown shell glued on top. It looked like a bearded wizard, with a mussel for his robes. He held a match-stick sized piece of driftwood. Painted on the bottom was "You Shell Not Pass!"

"He's a big Lord of the Rings fan."

"Wonderful. I can tell that sir has excellent taste. That's seven quid. But I'll throw in 'Seas the Day' for ten."

"Nice." I kind of wanted one of the stupid things for myself by that point, so that worked out. I picked up the two shell sculptures and headed for the counter.

The girl nodded at my mask. "I heard more people in London still wear those."

"A few. I just, you know, don't want to give anyone anything. Flu can be just as deadly for the immunocompromised."

*Like Meera.*

I swallowed down the memory and took a deep breath. The girl at the counter watched me closely. I expected a cynical look. I usually got that. People thought I was being paranoid. But there was something else in her expression, a kind of sympathy.

No, more than that: understanding. Like she could see my guilt, and she got it.

I pulled myself together. I was totally projecting.

"By the way, I don't suppose you know of anywhere that's hiring?"

"You could try the burger place next door. Imani owns this place and that, and she's been complaining that they're short-staffed."

"Like Gandalf."

She looked blank.

"Short-staffed?" I pointed at the small shell sculpture and Gandalf's tiny piece of wood, feeling like an idiot. But she laughed. A big, unselfconscious belly laugh.

"That is seriously terrible."

"Puns are contagious. I should leave six feet between myself and these things. Thanks for the tip. I'll check it out."

She rang up the sale. My gaze fell on the "Seas the Day" sculpture I'd just bought.

"Look, um, I'm Ajay."

"I'm Oleander."

"Like I said, I'm new here …"

Her phone buzzed as a notification appeared on the screen.

*Rupert: I'll pick you up at 7.*

Great. She had a boyfriend.

"So … I'll probably see you around," I finished, embarrassed.

"I hope so," Oleander said. "Good luck with the job hunt."

Oleander had been right about Imani being short-staffed. It had been unusually warm that March, bringing tourists to Southcliff earlier than usual. Imani had been working the fryer herself when I came in. She almost hugged me when I asked if they were hiring and said I could start the next day. Pa was insufferably smug that he'd been right about that in-person job hunting thing when I told him.

As soon as I got my first break, I wandered next door to Oleander's shop, bringing some chips to say thanks. Oleander was sitting behind the counter, and I thought I saw her wiping at her eyes as she looked up. But as she saw me, a smile appeared on her face.

"Oh hey, Ajay. Back for more shell puns?"

I'll admit, I was glad she'd remembered my name.

"I got a job at Burgerlicious."

"That's brilliant! Welcome to Imani's team. She's a great boss."

"Thanks for suggesting I ask her. That means I owe you chips. Which is literally the least I can do because I get them free when I'm working. Which is every weekend." I held up the greasy paper bundle.

"You get them free?" Oleander asked slowly.

"Yeah."

"So, you could, in theory, get them free every Saturday and bring them here?"

I was glad my mask hid just how wide my smile got at that. "I'll see what I can do."

# CHAPTER FIVE

## OLEANDER

Two of the unicorn floaties have been brought into the gift shop from outside. They fill most of an aisle. Ajay lounges in one, Oleander in the other, a heap of chips unwrapped between them, with pools of mayo and ketchup for dipping on the greasy paper. Late spring rain patters fiercely against the window, keeping the tourists away.

"Chips make work better," Oleander says.

"Chips are work. Unicorns make work better." Ajay pulls down his mask to pop another chip in his mouth. He's not perfect-looking, like Rupert. His eyebrows are too bushy, and his hair is overdue for a cut. But she likes the way his eyes crinkle when he grins.

"They should have unicorns in restaurants. Why don't they have unicorns in restaurants?"

"We should start a unicorn restaurant."

"That only serves chips." Oleander grabs another and eats. Ajay is smiling, watching her. She covers her mouth. "Sorry. I have rubbish table manners, I know. Rupert's always reminding me."

"Firstly, I don't think you do. Secondly, we have no table. You have excellent chip-shop-paper-on-floor manners."

Oleander laughs, then looks at the empty paper. "Where did all the chips go?"

"The unicorns have been nicking them."

"So that's why there's no unicorns in restaurants."

Ajay nods, sagely. "Back to the drawing board on that idea."

Oleander screws up the messy paper, and lobs it overhead, landing it perfectly in the bin behind the counter.

"Nice one."

Oleander nods, satisfied. "Dad and I used to play basketball a lot when I was younger."

"You don't anymore?"

"He's dead."

Ajay freezes. "Sorry. I didn't know."

Oleander shrugs. "I hadn't told you."

Ajay nods. His Adam's apple bobs. It's the same swallow she saw when he first came in, when she asked him about his mask. She knows that swallow. She can feel it in her own throat.

"Who did you lose?" she blurts out before she can stop herself. He turns to her, eyes wide.

"The mask," Oleander says, pointing at it. "You lost someone you loved to a disease. You don't have to tell me. But … I know how it feels to lose someone, if that helps."

Ajay looks at her, and she meets his dark eyes and holds his gaze. He seems to be considering. After a moment he nods.

"Meera, my little sister. She had a lot of health issues, and it seemed like we spent half her life in hospitals: transplants, experimental treatments, the works. She was doing well but was immunosuppressed. We full-on shielded right through the pandemic to make sure she was okay."

His voice catches, but he continues. "I got careless after everyone got vaccinated and went back to normal. I thought we'd made it. Went to see the footie with my mates. Woke with a sore throat, thought it was from the shouting. I was negative on a rapid test, too. So I didn't worry about it and hung out with Meera."

He closes his eyes and shakes his head.

"She got a fever a few days later, not COVID, just regular flu. Went downhill fast. She was given oxygen, ventilated." Ajay pauses. "None of it helped."

Oleander wants to reach over, wants to touch his hand. "It's not your fault."

Ajay shakes his head. "Everyone says that. Doesn't make it true."

She knows exactly what he means. "You can't let yourself accept that. It would feel selfish. Like letting yourself off the hook or betraying Meera."

"Yeah." He's looking at her, eyes wide.

"But it really isn't your fault."

He swallows, again. "You blame yourself for your dad's death?"

Oleander nods. "That was my fault. He killed himself."

"That doesn't sound like your fault."

"He was reaching out to me. I cut him off."

She hesitates, but there's understanding in Ajay's eyes. It's the expression she didn't realize she was looking for, with her mother, with Tisha, with Rupert.

"Dad ... had trouble since his girlfriend left him. I tried to help, to listen and that. But it got too much. He kept calling. Kept sending me messages."

She puts a hand to her forehead. Rubs, as if that could ease the memory. "I'd been replying less and less. The night before he … I had to study for an exam. I told him I was turning my phone off. When I turned it on the next day, there were dozens of messages. Angry messages, saying he needed me, saying I was selfish. The last one said if he couldn't count on me, he couldn't count on anyone. I called him, but he didn't answer."

Why hadn't she been kinder? Why hadn't she replied that night? She knew he'd been struggling.

The next memory is there. It's always there, too close. Some memories are too sharp to hold. Some memories are shrapnel, burying themselves deep within, bursting into everyday life unexpectedly, erupting into agony, time and time again. Some memories will reopen wounds, will not allow them to heal.

This memory is one of those.

She couldn't concentrate in her exam. They let people leave when they'd finished. She knew she'd failed, so she handed the paper in half-done and left with the smug smart kids. She turned her phone back on, desperate to hear from him, desperate to know he was okay.

She scrolled through her notifications. None were from him.

Her father's house was a short bus ride from the school, through residential streets clustered with mock-Tudor houses. She felt like she was going to be sick with every bump in the road. It felt like the bus was driving too slowly, as if it was taunting her.

She ran from the bus stop to her father's modern house, all sharp rectangles and white walls. She tried at the front door first. Rang the bell, then knocked on the solid white front door, hitting hard enough to split her knuckles.

"Dad!"

The house was silent. She stepped back, looking to see if there was movement at the wide windows. That's when she saw the smoke, coiling out from under the garage door.

She started running before she had time to think. Dashed to the side door of the garage, tried the handle and almost stumbled in as it opened into the dark. Oleander coughed on the fumes, panicking, but still thinking enough to hit the button to open the garage door. It rose, revealing the car, inch by inch as the light penetrated the mist. The sound of the engine thrumming filled the space. The blue car and the man in the front seat were revealed as the exhaust rolled out of the garage and onto the suburban street.

"Dad!" He was slumped over the wheel.

Oleander reached for the driver's door. She tugged it open with her free hand.

"Dad!"

His lips were pale. His eyes were closed. Oleander reached in and grabbed the keys from the ignition, silencing the hum. "Dad!"

She put her hands around him, checking for breath, for pulse, then fumbling for her phone.

She already knew it was too late.

In the gift shop, she takes a long, shaky breath. "He killed himself in his garage. I found him."

It's all she can manage to get out.

Ajay exhales a long breath and swears. He shakes his head. "Wasn't your fault. At all. He made his own choices."

Oleander shrugs. "I could have stopped it."

"Could you, though? No offense, but it sounds like he needed professional help, not you."

"You sound like Tish."

"Tish?"

"Tisha Jones. You must have seen me with her at school."

He raised a hand up to near his brow. "Tall girl? Rainbow hoodie?"

"That's the one."

"Maybe you should listen to her."

"But he wouldn't see a therapist. He wasn't that kind of man."

"He really shouldn't have put that on you."

"But he did, so I was the only person who could have helped. If I'd answered his messages that night, when he was at his lowest, I could have stopped it."

"I think you need to stop focusing on that day. My parents are always talking about the times Meera made us laugh, and my therapist tells me not to obsess about Meera's death, but to think about her life. Tell me something good about your dad. I'm guessing you don't get much of a chance to share that stuff."

"Yeah. Mum doesn't want to hear it. But Dad wasn't as bad as she makes him out to be." She feels her shoulders relax slightly. "He loved puns, like on those shell sculptures. He'd tell the longest, worst jokes, too. Painfully long, and never worth the punchline." She laughs.

Ajay's smiling too.

"And he hated mushrooms. Like, he was personally offended by then. He wouldn't even call them mushrooms, just fungi, or if he was particularly annoyed, 'spore-bearing fruiting bodies,' as in 'why are there spore-bearing fruiting bodies on my pizza?'"

She shakes her head. "I miss him, you know."

Ajay nods. "Yeah. I know."

She takes a long breath through her nose. "So, tell me about your sister. The good memories."

Ajay tips his head back. "Where to start? She was awesome. She never used to stop talking. Ever. She fell asleep mid-sentence sometimes when she was really little. It was hilarious." He runs a hand through his dark hair. "She had oxygen tubes in her nose sometimes. She'd call it her moustache. I used to worry about her all the time. We all did, but she never worried, not for a second.

"On long car rides she'd fall asleep the second we were on the road and hang forward in her seatbelt like an unconscious parachutist. I used to watch her chest, make sure she was breathing. But she was always fine. Until she wasn't."

He closes his eyes for a long moment. Water glistens on his dark eyelashes.

"Would you get rid of it, if you could? The regret?" she asks.

He sighs. "I guess. Never really thought about it. Would you?"

She nods without hesitating. It's hard to take the next breath. Whenever she thinks about that day, she's right back there, heart stuttering, hot and cold at the same time.

He reaches out and touches her arm. She pauses, and looks at his fingers on her skin, interrupting the memory.

"But you can't let the regret blot out the good stuff, you know? And for the record, your dad is totally right about mushrooms. They're slimy and gross." He gives a theatrical shudder.

She laughs, in spite of herself.

"Do you … visit your sister's grave and that?"

"She doesn't have one. We scattered her ashes in the Thames. But we do things to remember her, like raising money in her name for the food bank. I think she'd like that. She was always sharing her food. Well, mainly offloading her veggies onto my plate while Pa and Amma weren't looking, but you get the idea. Doing something for her makes me feel better." He pauses. "Maybe you could do something in your dad's memory, something that would make him happy."

She nods, considering. "He liked historic buildings and architecture. He took me to a lot of stately homes when I was little. Most were dull as hell, but I liked the ones with mazes. Maybe I could do some volunteering or fundraising or something. I think he'd like that."

"And I'm guessing he has a grave, since you asked about Meera's. Do you go there much?"

She gives a quick shake of her head. "Not since the funeral. I mean to, but …" She's not sure how she can explain it, that feeling of guilt for not visiting her dad battling with the impossibility of the idea of sitting at the headstone, alone apart from the memory of that day.

"I'm not sure I could face it on my own. Mum's offered to go with me, but she'd keep checking I was okay while trying to hide her contempt for him. I just …" She trails off.

"I could go with you. I mean, if it would help."

She glances up at him. His look is genuine. He really would go with her.

Her phone buzzes.

She glances at it. A part of her still hopes to see a message from her father. Still wishes this whole thing was just a nightmare. But once again, she's disappointed.

"I have to reply to this."

"Rupert, right?" Ajay's voice is flat.

She nods and reads the message.

*Julia was an utter cow this morning.*

Julia is Rupert's housemate. She's always on his back about something. Oleander tries not to be jealous that he lives with a woman his own age. She's determined not to say anything about it. Oleander wants to be a cool, no-drama girlfriend. Not a nag or a cow like Julia.

*Sounds awful,* Oleander replies. *Don't know how you put up with her.*

*Neither do I! But it helps to talk to you*
*Thx.*

She can see Ajay out of her peripheral vision. He's pulled his own phone out and is scrolling through something. He never complains when she messages Rupert.

Her phone buzzes again.

*By the way, I'm going to take you for a special trip up to London next Saturday.*

Oleander stares at the message for a moment before replying.
*So sorry. Working.*

*It's your birthday! Call in sick.*

She pauses before replying, feeling a little guilty.
*Can't let my boss down.*

*He'll be fine for one day. It's not like you're saving lives or anything.*

*Thx so much, but she ...* She hasn't even finished typing before the next message bubble pops up.

*Please? I've already booked it, and it's quite expensive. I just want to do something nice for you. You deserve it.*

Oleander pauses for a long moment. She sighs and deletes her half-formed message.

*Of course. Sorry. Sounds gr8.*

*You're going to love it! I promise. It's going to be so special.*

A chill runs through her, at those words, although she doesn't know why.

"Things okay?" Ajay says, once she puts away her phone.

"Um … yes. Fine," she lies.

# CHAPTER SIX

## AJAY

The last time I saw Oleander seemed super weird at the time.

Like I'd told her mum, it had been during the July heat wave. I'd been taking a shortcut through the car park behind Tesco and was regretting it. There was no shade, and the sun reflected off the cars and the tarmac, magnifying the already ridiculous midday heat. My mask was damp with sweat, totally gross.

You couldn't miss Oleander. She was the kind of girl who would catch your eye even without her purple hair. Which was just as well, as on that day her hair was pulled back into a tight bun.

My stomach lurched as I spotted her behind a red Kia one row over. I'd been hoping I'd run into her. I'd had a dozen conversations in my head with her, but now she was really there, I didn't know what to say.

I shouldn't say anything, I realized. She'd asked me to leave her alone.

I couldn't read the look that passed over her face when she caught sight of me. I'd always been rubbish at interpreting her expressions and head-tilts. It was like trying to understand a foreign language.

I put my head down and kept walking. I didn't want to get in her face. But she hurried between the cars to me and grabbed my wrist. Her touch sent a jolt through me.

"It wasn't you," she said.

"What?"

"It wasn't anything you did, you know, when I said we couldn't be friends anymore. I just want you to know that. I loved hanging out with you at the shop. Those were some of the best times I've had this year."

"Right," I said, confused.

"Like, I wish …" She shook her head. "I wish things could have been different. But it wasn't you. You've been nothing but great."

I looked down, totally thrown, and noticed writing scrawled up her arms in blue ink: an island name, something French-sounding.

"What's that?"

"What?" She looked at where I was pointing, and it was as if the words on her skin caught her by surprise. She read the name out, twice, as if to make it stick in her head.

"I keep forgetting. You know how terrible my memory is."

"I do?"

She looked a little sad. "I'm crap at remembering things. Like when I'm meant to be meeting people, promises I've made, that kind of thing."

"I've never noticed."

"Rupert says I have a terrible memory."

"Nah. That's not right."

She pointed at her arms. "Then why can't I remember about this?"

"About what?"

She checked her wrist again. "THIS. This island."

"Where is it?"

She swore under her breath. "Got it written down somewhere. One sec." She pulled out a notebook from her pocket and scanned it, flicking through handwritten notes. "Just off the coast, apparently."

She was acting weird, but I was glad to see her. I tried to keep up my end of the conversation. "Never heard of it."

"That's the thing, isn't it? I've never heard of it either."

"You lost me."

"Look," she dug out her phone. She pulled up the photo on her lock screen and tilted it toward me. The sun reflected off it, blinding me for a moment. I blinked and put a hand up.

"Sorry." She adjusted it, so I could see. It took a moment for me to be able to focus after being dazzled, and it was hard to make out the screen properly on the bright day, but the picture was obviously of her, when she was little, with an older man.

"Is … was that your dad?"

She nodded and smiled sadly at the picture.

"We went there when I was six. But I don't remember it."

"So? It was a long time ago, right?"

She looked unsure, so different from the unselfconscious girl I'd met in the Treasure Chest in March. "Could you do me a favor?"

"Of course," I said.

She pointed to the phone again. "Check out the place name." She leaned close enough for me to catch her smell through my mask; vanilla and something I didn't recognize. She pointed at a signpost behind the two of them. "Read it?"

I leaned in, squinting, and nodded.

She took the phone back, stuck her written-on arms behind her back and looked at me with a challenge in her eyes.

"What's the island called?"

There had always been something about her that threw me into a kind of confusion. Seeing her after not speaking for weeks took my tongue. And she was looking at me so intently, as if the world hinged on what I was about to say. I opened my mouth to reply but under the spotlight of her gaze and the bright sun, the name wouldn't come. I scrunched up my forehead.

"Sorry. Show me it again."

Her eyes widened. "You see? It's not just me, is it?"

It was as if a little light kindled in her. A bit of the old Oleander. She smiled. "Okay. Here's the deal. I'll show you the photo again if you can tell me one thing about what the island looked like. What could you see behind me and my dad?"

Again, I tried to focus on what had been in the picture. It was hard with her right there and everything I wanted to say threatening to choke me. Plus, I was sweating buckets, and hoping she couldn't smell it.

"Can't remember." I felt so stupid, but my confusion seemed to delight her.

"Thank you!" Oleander said, laughing. "It's not just me!"

If it had made her happy, I'd gladly have forgotten anything she wanted, a thousand times over.

I noticed more words, scrawled in the same blue ink over her other arm, saying things like "photo on phone," "notes" and "remember," and the island's name again. Then she grabbed me and hugged me tightly. I was too surprised to move as she pressed her cheek against my chest.

"That's it. I'm going to do it. Wish me luck!"

"Do what?"

"I'm off to find a goddess!"

"What?"

She stopped and faced me, face suddenly serious. "Look, Ajay, if it all gets too much, you know, the memories, the regrets, come find me, okay?"

"I … okay?"

"Take care, Ajay!" Then she was gone, hurrying across the baking hot carpark and down the side of Tesco.

# CHAPTER SEVEN

## OLEANDER

The hotel room is luxurious, the carpet thick and soft. A picture window shows the hubbub of Piccadilly Circus bathed in summer sunshine many floors below.

Rupert holds the door open and waves Oleander in. She steps into the room, hesitantly.

"Wow. This place is gorgeous. I'm so sorry though, I can't stay over or anything. I told Mum …"

"Don't worry, don't worry," Rupert bustles in behind her. "I promised I would return you by eleven, and I will keep that promise."

She drifts over to the window, admiring the view. "Then why have you got a hotel room?"

Rupert rummages in the room's mini-fridge and pulls out a bottle of champagne.

"London is so exhausting, don't you think? I always want a little rest while I'm here. I booked this so we could have a break and a toast. To us, and to your seventeenth birthday."

He unwraps the cork and pops it out of the bottle. Oleander jumps at the noise.

"Can you grab the glasses from the bathroom?"

Oleander does as she's asked. Rupert pours the wine into the two water glasses and hands her one. He perches on the edge of the king-sized bed.

"Sit, my little Clara Bow." He pats the spot next to him.

Oleander joins him, smiling at the nickname. She likes not being Oleander Dillon. She takes the offered glass and sips.

Rupert turns to her, eyes intense. "I know we've not been together that long, but I've felt strongly about you from the moment we met." He pulls a flat box from the bag he's been carrying. "I got this for you."

He opens the box. Inside is a long, multi-strand silver and pearl necklace on a bed of velvet. Oleander lifts it carefully. It looks like something that should be in a museum.

"Do you like it?"

"It's gorgeous. Just … amazing."

He beams. "It's a real antique. I wanted to get you a necklace that Clara Bow herself would have worn. You have such a classic beauty, and I thought this would help bring it out."

He takes the necklace and puts it around her neck. She stares down at it, hanging over her black dress. It seems too expensive for her to just wear. She's not the kind of girl who has anything like this.

She tries to fight the feeling that she doesn't deserve it.

He runs a finger over the chain on her skin, then kisses her neck, working down to where the lowest part hangs, in the dip of her low-cut dress. His kisses tickle.

He leans on her, kissing harder and pushing her gently down onto the bed, hand sliding along her leg.

She lies back stiffly, trying not to spill her drink. "Hang on. Um."

Rupert pulls back. "Oh, I'm sorry. I don't want to pressure you, of course."

She sits up and takes a large sip of her wine, trying to relax.

"We don't have to do anything," Rupert says.

"Thanks," she says, and knocks back some more of the wine, too fast. It fizzes on the inside of her nose, making her want to sneeze. She looks down at the necklace again. It really is beautiful.

"I just wanted it to be special when I said it for the first time." He takes the glass from her and puts it on the side. He clasps her hands, pulling her toward him.

"I know it's early, but I've never met anyone like you. You're so special, Oleander, and I don't think you even realize it. I love you, Oleander."

She nods, trying to focus on how Rupert makes her feel: like someone else. Like someone special, someone who would deserve this necklace.

Rupert waits.

"I love you too."

Rupert squeezes her hands so tight it hurts. "It means so much to me to hear you say it. I can't tell you how nervous I've been!" He gives a little laugh.

"You were nervous?" She stares at the beautiful man in front of her. How could he be nervous around a screw-up like her?

"Absolutely! You have no idea of the effect you have on me." The way he looks at her fills her with gratitude. She wants to be the girl she sees in his eyes: sophisticated and beautiful, his Clara Bow.

He starts kissing her again. "I can barely keep control of myself," he says, into her neck. "That's your influence."

After a few more long kisses, he presses her gently back down onto the bed again, running his hands over her.

She feels bad, for not being as crazy about him as he is about her. He's smart, handsome, and generous. Why can't she fall for him? What's wrong with her? She thinks of what another girl would do. A girl who wasn't Oleander. The girl Rupert sees her as. A girl who does the right things, who makes other people happy.

Oleander is just as stiff as before, but this time, she doesn't say anything.


Afterwards, Oleander sits on the bed facing the window, while Rupert showers. She pours herself more wine. When Rupert comes back with a towel around his waist, he gestures at the bathroom, so she stands to take her turn in the shower, sheet clutched against her, feeling awkward, dizzy from the alcohol and not as different as she'd hoped.

Rupert grabs the blanket, playfully, pulling her against him. He kisses her and runs his hand down her naked back.

"I love you," he says.

"I love you too." She doesn't pause this time.

He keeps hold of the sheet when she eventually pulls away. Oleander grabs at it, but he doesn't let go, so she gives up and scurries naked toward the bathroom, giggling. When she's nearly there, a flash lights the room for a split second.

Oleander turns back. Rupert holds his phone by his side.

She is confused, lost for a moment. She feels as if she's trying to put something together that doesn't fit.

"Did you ... did you just take a picture of me?"

"No."

"I thought I saw a flash."

Rupert shakes his head. "No flash in here."

"Can I see your phone?"

Rupert lifts his phone. The screen is black. "Maybe it was the lights. Sometimes that happens if there's a power surge. I probably just blinked and missed it."

Oleander stands still, arms across her body protectively.

"Don't you trust me, my Clara Bow?" Rupert asks.

She shakes her head, trying to clear it of the doubt the wine has brought. She smiles.

"Sorry. Yes, of course I do."

# CHAPTER EIGHT

## AJAY

It was well cold on the walk home from Sarah's house. I pulled my shirt down over the writing on my arm. A paper bag skimmed along the pavement caught by the wind. I watched it trying to catch flight until it landed in the gutter and crumpled into a puddle, damp spreading through it.

What had I just been thinking about? It was something important, I knew that. Something to do with Oleander, and with my arm too. I glanced down at my left arm, and saw the blue ink on my wrist, peeking out from my shirt.

The hair stood up on the back of my neck. I didn't remember what I'd written. I rolled up my sleeve, bit by bit, revealing each letter. It was my handwriting, but I didn't remember what it said. It was only once I saw the full island's name it all clicked into place.

This was so weird.

I pushed my sleeve down again and turned the name of the island over in my head, as a test: Levay Island, Levay Island, Levay Island. I could keep it there by repeating it.

A car cut too close to the curb, hitting the puddles there. I leapt back to avoid the splash. It barely got my trainers, but I moved away from the edge of the pavement in case it happened again, then tried to remember what I'd been thinking about before the car.

Something to do with my arm. Something I wanted to remember.

I glanced down and went through it all again. This time I pulled my phone out, and opened the Notes app, ready to put it in there, and perhaps set alarms to remind myself. But there, right at the top of the screen was a new note: Levay Island.

Again, a chill for a second before I remembered. Right, I'd already put it in my phone the last time I'd been through this weird pantomime. If I kept it in my head, it stayed there, complete; the photo, the Post-it in Oleander's room, the writing on her arms and mine, all of it. But I didn't seem to be able to hold on to the memory, once it wasn't front-of-mind.

I felt like a total Muppet.

As soon as I got home I dodged Pa and Amma by shouting that I was going to do homework. I ran up to my room, took my mask off and wrote "LEVAY ISLAND" in big letters on a sheet of paper and stuck it right in the middle of my wall where I couldn't miss it.

It was totally weird. My memory of other stuff seemed fine, far as I could tell. I ran a few tests of random things: our old address in London, a couple of my passwords, French verb conjugations I'd been working on for school. They were all there. Well, the verb conjugations were hazy, but that was normal. It was just the island that wouldn't stay in my head. I would have thought I was losing it, if I hadn't seen the evidence Oleander had done exactly what I was doing.

I was starting to understand her the last time I saw her. Why she'd written over her arms. Why she'd slapped Post-its on all her photos. She'd been checking her memory, seeing if it was just the island she forgot, or other places too. She'd been doubting herself.

And I remembered something she'd said, back when she was still talking to me.

*What if you could forget and be forgotten? Not blow a hole in people's lives, like Dad did, but just slip away?*

I got why a forgotten island would appeal to a girl like Oleander. I glanced at the framed picture of Meera grinning on my desk. I'd dealt with my regret a different way, focusing on the good things, grieving with my parents, and seeing a therapist for the stuff I didn't want to talk about with them. It wasn't perfect. Even I could see the appeal of forgetting. Oleander couldn't grieve with her mum and had no one to share the happy memories with, so the draw of something like that would be so much stronger for her.

A gentle knock came at the door.

"Yes?"

It opened, and Amma peered in. I saw her face relax as she saw the handwritten notes next to my laptop, and I wondered if she was checking I'd been telling the truth about doing homework. I gestured at the island's name on my wall.

"Local history assignment."

Amma nodded. "Good boy. Did you want anything to eat? Or tea and biscuits?"

I leaned back in my chair. Amma had left her job as a pharmacist to look after Meera, and although she was working again these days, seemed a bit adrift without my sister to care for.

"Tea would be nice. Thanks."

I saw her gaze catch on the photo of Meera before she left the room. She paused.

"Remember how she hated tea?" I said. "Called it mud-water?"

Amma laughed. "She'd even complain about the smell of it on my breath."

She looked back at me, and we shared a sad smile before she slipped out of my room, closing the door behind her.

You can't just be forgotten, no matter what Oleander wanted. It doesn't work like that. If Oleander had thought she could be forgotten, she'd been wrong. She'd blown a hole in people's lives anyway. Her mother's, for a start, and mine too.

I saw the paper with "LEVAY ISLAND" across it taped on my wall, remembered what I was doing and resumed my search online. I was wondering if it was even a real place. I doubted I'd find anything, but there were thousands of pages of results.

It was everywhere you'd expect it to be: Google Maps, Wikipedia, tourist sites and blogs, and there was a long article about historic buildings threatened by climate change that I could only read a bit of because of a paywall. The most recent review on TripAdvisor had been posted in May, a couple of months before Oleander went missing. Then there were no more mentions of the island anywhere; not even something saying it had been closed to the public. I checked again. I used Twitter and sorted by "latest." But no matter how I looked, there was nothing after May.

It was as if the island had stopped existing one day in the spring and no one noticed because everyone forgot about it at the same time.

It was so messed up.

I made a ton of notes, but it didn't matter how much I learned, the moment I looked away, Levay Island slipped right out of my mind.

If I whispered the name over and over, kept researching, or said it silently in my head, it was okay. But the second I was distracted, it vanished. I did some reading on short-term and long-term memory, and with a few experiments learned that Levay would only stay in my short-term memory. It wouldn't move to long-term memory. That was a sign of certain kinds of brain damage, apparently. But I wasn't forgetting anything else.

It wasn't me that was the problem, it was the island.

Oleander had been through this too. That's why she'd checked the photo with me. That's why she was so happy when I couldn't remember either. I'd confirmed she wasn't mad.

I should have paid attention. I should have listened better. I shouldn't have been so bloody worried about looking like an idiot. I should have asked her more about the island.

Now she was my guide. She'd gone down this path too. I had to follow her.

I made a master sheet with short points on it. Levay was a tiny island, under ten hectares, whatever that meant, located a few miles out from Southcliff Beach, where Oleander and I had worked. It had nothing much on it except a manor which, like the island itself, belonged to some rich family that had lived there for centuries. There had been Iron Age remains found there, and rumors of a lost Roman temple. The house was built on the ruins of a monastery. It was pretty; high cliffs surrounded much of the island and it was home to rare sea birds. One of the two beaches had a pier for boats to moor.

I wrote everything down, trying to make it stick. I was proud of myself, like a hard-boiled detective in a movie, trying to find the dame, tracing her last known steps.

It wasn't hard to work out how Oleander had found out about the forgotten island. I'd seen her looking at photos of her dad on her phone all the time. She had an album she'd made on there. She must have noticed the sign for Levay and couldn't remember it. If she hadn't been so obsessed with those pictures, if she hadn't gone back to them so often, she'd never have noticed she was forgetting the island. Her mind probably slid off it dozens of times, maybe hundreds before she realized what was happening.

Perhaps she took the picture to her mother, to Rupert, to her friends, and tried the trick she pulled on me. She got hold of a book about the island somehow too. She'd been reading it in the gift shop when I'd come by a few times. I'd thought it was something for school, as she'd filled it with tabs and highlights. I couldn't remember what was on the cover or what it was about; my mind slipped off it, just like it did the island.

I hadn't seen the book in Oleander's room, so perhaps it was still at the gift shop. I should go and check. Perhaps her notes would explain more.

I knew I should tell Oleander's mum what I'd found out, but I was kind of scared of her. Sarah already thought I'd helped Oleander run away to London. If I came to her with a wild story about an island no one could remember, she'd call the cops on me. I didn't rate my chances of explaining any of this to them, especially not with a white lady basically accusing me of trafficking her daughter. There was no way of explaining any of it to *anyone* without it sounding like I was losing it. No wonder Oleander hadn't tried.

Still, I wished she'd trusted me. I wished she hadn't cut me out of her life.

That was another issue. Oleander had asked me to leave her alone, but later, she'd told me to find her if the memories got too much. I had no idea which of those she really meant. Would she want me to try to find her?

There was only one person who might know the answer: her best friend, Tisha Jones.

# CHAPTER NINE

## OLEANDER

Oleander and Tisha sit back from the fading white lines that mark the edge of the college football pitch, staying out of the way of the game.

"Seriously?" Tisha says.

Oleander nods, plucking at the over-long grass, picking the fattest blades and letting the breeze catch them as they fall to the ground. "Seriously."

"You didn't tell me you were going to!"

"I didn't know I was going to."

"Sounds amazing."

"It was okay."

"You lost your virginity in a luxury London hotel room, drinking champagne after he gave you a crazy expensive antique necklace, you both confessed your love and it was okay?"

"I mean, I guess it was better than okay."

Tisha waves a hand. "Totally beats under the slide in Southcliff Park with a few cans of White Claw."

Oleander looks up. "Alex Black, right? You had such a crush on them."

"You know it. No regrets. They're fit as you like." Tisha tilts her head. "But why don't you seem happy about it? You love him, right?"

"I told him I loved him."

"Did you mean it?"

Oleander pauses. "I really like him. He's gorgeous, and so generous, and it's only a matter of time before I'm properly in love with him, right?"

Tisha shakes her head. "I have no idea how you are resisting that rich boy charm. He's so hot and takes you on mad romantic dates."

"Yeah, but I wish we could do normal things too, like hang out at his place and play video games. I get why we can't, but still." She pauses. "And he wants me to dye my hair back to brown."

Tisha reaches out for a curl that's escaped Oleander's bun. "I like your purple hair."

"Yeah, me too. I've been putting it up for now. Rupert says it looks really classy like this."

"You shouldn't dye your hair back if you don't want to. Not even for Hottie McLawyer. There are other guys."

Oleander nods, glancing across the field, as if looking for someone. "I suppose."

Tisha leans in. "Look, you know you don't have to stay with him just because you slept with him, right? Even if it was your first time. It's not like that makes you married or something."

Oleander puts a shocked hand to her chest. "It doesn't? But he took my virtue!"

"Seriously, if he wants you to change, maybe you're just not right for each other."

"But there's loads of stuff I want to change about myself. And I totally want to be classier."

"But that's got to come from you. Keep your hair if you like it."

She nods, thoughtfully. "Thanks, Tish. I'll talk to him."

# CHAPTER TEN

## AJAY

When I messaged Tisha to ask if we could talk about Oleander, she replied in seconds. We both had a free period that afternoon, so we met in the canteen. Even though lunch was long over, there was the usual clamor of students eating on their own schedule, the screech of chairs being pushed out from tables, and the background burble of various too-loud conversations.

We found a table in the corner, the noise of the space providing its own kind of privacy.

"Do you know where she's gone?" Tisha asked, the moment we sat down.

"I'm not sure," I said. "I have an idea, but I wanted to ask if she'd want me to look."

Tisha tilted her head. "What do you mean?"

"She could be … confusing. She basically told me to never talk to her again, then just before she left, she told me to find her if I needed to."

Tisha's jaw set. "Rupert."

"Her boyfriend?"

"Yeah, if you can call him that."

"What?"

"He's the reason why she told you to leave her alone, I bloody guarantee you. He's the reason she stopped talking to me."

I leaned back. "She stopped talking to you, too?"

"After Ollie told him I was queer. He 'didn't trust me around her,' apparently. And if he felt that way about me with a straight girl like her, I bet he was a billion times worse about you."

"Oh," was all I managed.

"Isolating their victim. Classic abuser tactic. Not that he hit her, as far as I know. He was way more subtle than that."

I felt dizzy. "I … I thought she was happy with him."

"Yeah. He fooled us all." She shifted in her chair, uncomfortably. "I mean he started out as a total dreamboy, you know? Taking her to all these fancy places, buying her super expensive stuff, drowning her in compliments, saying he was head over heels and all that."

She waved a hand. "Apparently that's a total tactic. 'Lovebombing' they call it. I had no idea. Ollie had no idea. Anyway, then he changed. Although I guess he didn't change, not really. The mask just slipped." She paused, face dark. "He must have spotted how vulnerable she was that first time he met her in his office."

"What did he do?"

"Criticized her. Small things at first. Ollie has always been way too self-conscious so she totally bought into the negging. Then he started gaslighting her. Whenever he was late or broke a promise, he said she'd misremembered the time, or he'd never said anything of the sort, that kind of thing. I think, because of her guilt over her dad, that on some level she thought she deserved it all."

I leaned back in my chair, feeling stupid.

"I should have been looking out for her, but I was so happy that she'd found something to take her mind off things. I didn't want to see the red flags." She shook her head, sadly. "You know about the photo, right?"

"Kind of. I didn't see it, but I heard things. A naked photo, right? People were sharing it."

Tisha nodded. "He took it the first time they had sex. When she started to talk about splitting up with him, he said he'd been hacked, and it had been leaked. He promised he'd use his lawyer muscles to get it offline. She was so upset about it all, and felt she had to stick with him while he got it sorted."

"Did he get it sorted?"

She shook her head. "No. And when she decided to leave him in spite of that, he told her he was suicidal, that he'd kill himself if she ended things."

I swore.

"Right? Scumbag knew her weaknesses. Knew she couldn't dump him because of her dad. She felt trapped, and she was getting bullied over the photo, too. I tried to help, tried to convince her to end it with him anyway, but he had his claws in too deep by then. She broke off contact with me then disappeared."

I felt disconnected from the canteen. Staccato laughter erupted at a table to my left. Trays clattered and people wandered through, necks craned as they looked for their friends, but it all felt like it was on the other side of thick glass.

"That's …" I couldn't come up with a word.

"Right? At least he's up to his neck in the brown stuff now. It's the only thing that makes me feel any better."

"Why? Is he a suspect or something?"

Tisha shook her head. "Had an alibi for when she went missing.

But the police looked into that photo thing after Ollie went missing, and it turns out he totally wasn't hacked at all. He posted it to some revenge porn site."

She leaned in, a wry smile on her face. "And guess what? Turns out, if you share a naked photo of an under-eighteen, that's technically child porn."

I almost smiled at that. "He's going down for child porn?"

Tisha nodded. "You'd think a solicitor, of all things, would have known better, right? And guess what else: he was engaged to the woman he lived with. He told Ollie she was some nutso roommate. Got his ass dumped pretty damn quick when that whole 'child porn' thing rolled in."

I nodded, trying to process the deluge of new information. I felt like a total idiot. I should have known what she was going through. Or had some kind of idea.

"So, do you think you know where she might be?"

"I … Did she ever show you a photo of her and her dad?"

"No, I don't think so. Why?"

I wished I could tell Tisha everything. But I'd sound like I'd lost it. "I just think that's where she might have gone."

"Where?"

I dropped my left arm to my lap, and subtly pushed back the sleeve.

"Levay Island," I read.

"Never heard of it."

"But before I go and look, I just wanted to check. Do you think she'd want to be found?"

Tisha paused. "Someone needs to find her, at least to check. The police asked if I thought she might be suicidal, and I don't think she was, but she wasn't okay at all."

"But should it be me?"

She looked up and held my gaze. "Yeah, I think of all people, she'd be okay with you. If you find her and she's good where she is, you'll walk away, right? I mean, you did that once before when she told you to leave her alone, right?"

I nodded.

"I don't need to know where she is. Her mother doesn't need to know where she is, and I can't lie to Sarah. All we need to know is that she's okay."

Tisha exhaled. "Please, find her if you can."

# CHAPTER ELEVEN

## OLEANDER

Oleander combs her fingers through her hair, trying to sort out her reflection in a tiny shell-rimmed mirror in the gift shop. She puts on some lip gloss and checks her watch. Every few seconds, her gaze flicks up toward the door at the back of the shop. The door to Burgerlicious.

When the front doorbell rings, she jumps, spinning around to greet the customer. But as he walks in, her smile freezes.

"Rupert!" she says, trying to push enthusiasm into her voice.

He strides down the aisle toward her counter. "Since this place steals you from me every weekend, I thought I'd come by and surprise you, take you out to lunch."

"Oh … you should have said you were coming. I don't know if I can."

"You get to take lunch with the shifts you do. I know employment law and —"

"I usually just have something here." She glances back toward the door to Burgerlicious.

"Then today's your lucky day, right?"

"I ... well ... I guess." She straightens up. "Actually, I wanted to talk to you about something, anyway."

Rupert looks apprehensive. "About what?"

"It's my hair, I —"

The back door of the shop creaks open. Ajay strides through. "Southcliff's finest chips. Pretty low bar, but still ... oh." He pauses, package still raised aloft, triumphantly.

Rupert looks from Ajay to Oleander, and back again. "Where did he come from?"

Ajay heads down the aisle, hand held out. "Rupert, right?"

Rupert just looks at Ajay's hand. "Are you the delivery boy?"

Ajay laughs. "Nice one. I'm Ajay. I work next door."

Rupert stares at him for a long moment. "Well, thanks then." He takes the chips from Ajay.

"Wait ..." Oleander says.

"It's okay," Ajay says, already backing up the aisle. "Don't want to interrupt. Catch you later, Oleander. Nice to meet you, Rupert."

He ducks out through the back door, wafting the scent of chip fat behind him.

Rupert turns back to Oleander as soon as he is gone. "He was leering at you."

"He was not. And how would you even tell, with the mask?"

"Who is he?"

"Ajay's just a mate. He works next door and brings me chips sometimes."

"He comes here while you're working? Why didn't you tell me about this?"

Oleander shrugs, feeling guilty. "Not much to tell."

"I don't want him coming here, hitting on you at work."

"He's not hitting on me. Anyway, he's just started at my school. Am I meant to avoid him there too?"

"He's in your school as well?" Rupert starts pacing up and down the aisle. "What else have you been keeping from me?"

"Keeping from you? Don't be ridiculous. It just never came up."

Rupert's jaw clenches. He clutches the chips tightly.

"I'm ridiculous, am I? Is that what you think of me? Ridiculous?"

He drops the bag on the counter, and walks away, shaking his head.

Oleander tries to think of something to say, but he's already out of the front door, the bell tinkling behind him.

# CHAPTER TWELVE

## AJAY

Sunday was one of those gloomy autumn days that remind you that winter's coming. I wore a waterproof jacket over a jumper Oleander had always liked; brown with patches on the shoulders that looks much cooler than it sounds. I folded one of the posters into the inside pocket, safe from the rain. I'd taken to carrying it with me, just in case.

My parents had gone to Bristol to visit Amma's cousin there. They'd asked me if I'd wanted to come but didn't really expect me to say yes. It was the perfect opportunity to look for Oleander's book. I took the bus down to Southcliff Beach. I checked the note on my hand a lot, as I kept forgetting what I was doing. Luckily, I was on autopilot, heading toward the place I'd worked.

The gift shop was part of a pastel-colored row of ice cream places, chippies, gift shops and pubs that ran along the seafront, a magnet for tandoori-red tourists in the summer. The pavements were empty now. The inflatable unicorns and plastic windmills were packed away. My work was shuttered for the off-season too, but I still had a key for the side door that I'd never got around to returning, and I knew the alarm signs on the window were a lie.

Burgerlicious was attached to the Treasure Chest through an office at the back of the building. My old boss, Imani, owned both businesses, so I slipped through there and into the darkened aisles of Oleander's shop. The aisles were blocked by the display stuff that usually sat outside; bins of sun hats and racks of T-shirts.

The Treasure Chest felt lifeless without Oleander there. This was her space, her little kingdom of tack. I'd spent so much time there with her. I'd kept that promise I'd made, about bringing her chips. We'd had lunch together every Saturday until one weekend in early July.

I could tell there was something not right that last day, as soon as I walked in. She was frowning at her phone, and her eyes were puffy, so involved in whatever was on the screen she didn't hear the back door open. Her hair was tied in a bun and tucked under her collar, hiding the purple.

I'd heard about the photo that was going around, but I'd been careful not to see it. She clearly didn't want it out there. A green book sat next to her, bristling with Post-it notes, and a notebook with a picture of her and her father on the cover lay beside it.

"Hi," I said, softly.

For a second, a smile twitched at the corner of her mouth. But her expression hardened.

I held up the bag of chips. "Lunch delivery."

She stiffened. "I … brought my own lunch today. I should try to be healthier."

"Oh, okay." I'd been wondering if I should be getting a few more vegetables in myself, but still, there was something off about her look.

"And I've given my notice."

The room felt a bit darker. "You're quitting?"

She nodded, and looked down at the counter. "And we should probably stop hanging out. Sorry, Ajay."

"Are you okay?"

"Ajay, you have to go."

I felt like I was falling. This wasn't like her. She still didn't look up.

"What's going on? Is this about ... Rupert and that photo?"

She winced, and I wished I hadn't said anything. "I haven't seen it, I promise. I just heard about it." I'd screwed things up, like the total idiot I was. "I'm sorry. I shouldn't have brought it up. I don't want to get in your face. But I'm here, okay? If you want to talk."

"Just ... forget about me, Ajay. I want everyone to forget about me."

She was scaring me. "What?"

Oleander looked up and met my gaze. "Would you get rid of your regrets, if you could?"

"What d'you mean?"

"What if you could forget and be forgotten? Not blow a hole in people's lives, like my dad did, but just slip away?"

"What's going on?" She shook her head, like I wasn't getting it. "I think you need some help, Oleander."

Her face changed. Her mouth became a line. "Just leave me alone, okay?"

It felt like a punch. I had to swallow a few times before I could get a reply out.

"Um ... Yeah. Sorry. I thought ... I really didn't mean to bug you."

I couldn't say anything else. I could barely keep it together, so I just did what she'd asked, and left the Treasure Chest.

I wandered to the counter at the back, wishing I'd known everything back then, wishing I'd done something differently. Perhaps I could have stopped her going.

The register was open, the drawer empty, like it always had been after Oleander cashed out. I knelt down, turned on my phone and used its light to search the shelves behind the counter. There were boxes of till rolls and stock, but among them, I noticed the spine of a green book.

I pulled it out. Yellow Post-its bristled between its pages.

*A History of Levay*

I didn't want to stay in the gift shop any longer than I had to, in case a passerby got the wrong idea when they saw a masked man in the dark, so I locked up quickly and took it to a nearby café. I ordered a black coffee and I sat as far away from other people as I could before I lowered my mask to take the first sip.

It was well-thumbed, with passages highlighted, underlined, and tabbed. How many times had I seen Oleander reading it and taking notes in the last weeks she'd worked there? But until I was holding it, it hadn't stayed in my head.

Weird. All of this was so weird.

I focused on the bits that Oleander had marked up the most. It looked like she'd been totally obsessed by the myth of the Lady of Levay, who was a misty, ghost-like woman who cropped up when bad stuff happened on the island. Those pages were covered with tabs, highlighted, and underlined. I read the first one.

*Few of the legends of the island have as much staying power as that of the Lady of Levay. The earliest evidence may come from the Iron Age, although it is possible that the surviving statuettes from this time may have been from an unrelated fertility cult.*

*The first reliable evidence for the worship of the Lady of Levay emerges in the Roman era when she appears as a protective goddess of the island. There are further hints of her in late antiquity, and she reappeared in the Middle Ages, worshipped by the ill-fated monks of the Levay Monastery.*

*The consistency in her appearance throughout all these incarnations — a misty apparition draped in robes of gray — and her association with doomed figures from the island's history has lent an extra dimension of risk and romance to her story.*

I flicked through sections on the early history of Levay and the Romans, and read about a heretical monastery who worshipped their own incarnation of the Virgin Mary. The monks were apparently the first to call her "the Lady of Levay."

After having no contact with the island for a while due to unusual weather conditions, a boat was sent out to check on them. The sailors found them all dead by starvation, save one, who ranted about being unable to reach the mainland and being controlled by a murderous abbot who trapped them there and forced them to build statues from his drawings. But the statues had been smashed, by the surviving monk, who continued to rave about mists and "the Lady."

So creepy.

The abbot's crimes turned out to be real; young novice nuns who had been placed under the abbot's care had never arrived at the convents to which they had been promised.

Oleander had highlighted the line about being unable to reach the mainland and on the yellow tab, in her handwriting, was a note that said "Fog? Forgotten by everyone else?"

Oleander obviously thought that whatever was going on with the island had happened before, hundreds of years ago.

I carried on reading. A whole passage was underlined on the next page.

*Although the story of the killings of the Abbot of Levay is too well-documented in the historical record to deny, there are many odd aspects. For example, most of the would-be nuns had been missing for years. They had not written to their families from their new convent homes, as would have been expected, yet no suspicions were raised until after the deaths at the monastery were discovered.*

Again, there was another yellow tab. On this one Oleander had written "forgotten nuns?"

Forgetting was a theme for Oleander, obviously. It cropped up again and again in her notes. She was particularly interested in a story about a Captain Granger who had married the daughter of an Earl of Levay but apparently cheated on her. She'd highlighted almost the whole story and scribbled in the margins. The book said the Earl had approached his daughter with evidence that the captain was "disreputable," but the Earl's daughter had quickly seemed to forgive and forget. Oleander had underlined, highlighted, and circled the word *forget.*

It was kind of overkill, but I got the point.

As I was reaching the end of the book, a folded piece of paper fell out.

I picked it up from the floor. It was a photocopy of a page from another book entirely, one on Greek mythology. The heading read:

*Lethe, Goddess of Forgetting*

There wasn't much on her, barely half a page. Lethe was a Greek goddess in some stories, but in others Lethe was a river that flowed through the underworld. There were more handwritten notes in Oleander's writing on the back, this time on *genius loci* and *lares;* spirits of a place, like local gods and goddesses.

It wasn't hard to put her thinking together.

Place names always got a bit mangled over the years, Londinium to London, Brycgstow to Bristol, we'd covered that in school. Oleander told me she was going to find a goddess. She obviously thought Lethe Island had become Levay Island; an island haunted by a local goddess of forgetting.

It must have seemed like an ideal place for a girl who wanted to forget and be forgotten. Did she think there really was a goddess there? One who could make her forget and be forgotten?

I felt the tug of the idea myself. I had some memories I would rather lose. Like my sister Meera in the hospital bed I put her in, hooked up to all the tubes that couldn't keep her alive.

I closed my eyes and swallowed. I had to focus on the good memories, like I'd been practicing. I thought about the time she learned how to make a fart noise with her armpit and her hand, and didn't stop doing it for like, a week and we were all begging her to quit. I smiled slightly, then my gaze fell down to my lap, and for a moment, I was surprised to see a book there.

I shook my head. I had to focus on what I was here for. I had to keep Levay in my mind.


It had stopped raining by the time I'd wandered down to the beach. Standing on the shore, I couldn't remember what I was doing, but I caught sight of the writing on my hand.

I peered out to sea, trying to work out where the island should be.

There was some low cloud over to the right, not too far away. I'd seen mist offshore before, but there was something weird about the fog bank. I wasn't a weatherman or anything, but it felt more and more wrong as the clouds cleared and the sun got brighter. What really gave it away was the fact that if I wasn't looking at it directly, I forgot the fog was even there.

It was for sure Levay Island, and it was tantalizingly close. I stood there for a while, staring at the cloud. It really didn't look that far.

I remembered what Oleander had said, the last time I saw her.

*If it all gets too much, you know, the memories, the regrets, come find me, okay?*

She'd meant my regrets about Meera. But I felt sick with regret when I thought of Oleander. I'd spent the last few months feeling like I'd let her down, that I should have listened better, that I could have done something to prevent her disappearance. Seeing the state her mother was in made it all worse. The regrets had got too much. It was time to do as she'd said and find her.

I just needed a boat.

I checked my watch; 12:40. It was ages until Pa and Amma would be back from Bristol. With a boat with a small engine, I could easily visit the island and be back before they were home. I pulled out a pen from my pocket and wrote a new note on the back of my hand.

*Rent boat. Go to Levay.*

# CHAPTER THIRTEEN

## OLEANDER

Oleander knew she looked mad as she hurried up the coast, muttering to herself under her breath.

"Get a boat, get to Levay, get a boat, get to Levay."

She should have brought a pen. She should have realized the ferry wouldn't be running. She'd been so stupid, just like she always was. Rupert wasn't wrong about that.

"Get a boat, get to Levay, get a boat, get to Levay."

She remembered the watersports center from when she was a child, when her father took her out for sailing lessons, before the divorce. But when she reached the main office, she saw it was shuttered. She cursed under her breath. It was coming up on evening, so she shouldn't be surprised. She shouldn't have spent so long waiting for a ferry that was clearly never going to come. Idiot, idiot, idiot.

"Get a boat, get to Levay." The rhythm of the phrase was stuck in her head, as much of a mental command now as an attempt to hold a memory. "Get a boat, get to Levay." And what else was there for her to do? Go home? She paced in front of the closed office.

"Get a boat, get to Levay."

But how?

Halyards clanged against masts, like off-key windchimes. The sound reminded her of coming to the center with her father, of the days they spent together. Dozens of boats were tied up alongside narrow docks; some of them were the bigger yachts that rich people kept here, but there were a few small Lasers, like the kind she and her dad used to take out together. She hurried over to one of those.

"Get a boat, get to Levay. Get a boat, get to Levay."

Those times seemed closer to Oleander, as she stood there. Her father had helped her learn how to sail one of these. She remembered him laughing when she tipped it the first few times, dunking them both in the sea. She remembered the taste of the salt, his grin as he righted the boat and his hand in hers as he heaved her back in. She'd felt so useless, but he told her it was all part of learning.

She kept muttering, "Get a boat, get to Levay," but she barely heard her own mantra. She could feel the memory of the warmth of an old, mild sunburn on her shoulder, where she'd missed a spot with the sunscreen. She could see her dad, the man he was years ago, before the divorce, before his break-up with Fiona, back when he smiled easily, and was so proud of her when she first took a boat out on her own. She could see the man who cheered her on from the dock, yelling through cupped hands over the glint of sunshine on water.

"Get a boat, get to Levay."

The ache wasn't as bad when she thought of those times. When he'd helped her to learn to sail, he was so different than the way he'd been in his last days. And it wasn't her fault he hadn't been that man anymore, was it? She'd just been a child when he'd started to change.

She paused, looking at the Laser. Maybe Ajay was right. Maybe focusing on the good memories did help. Maybe she could deal with this, step by step, with him, or on her own.

"Get a boat, get to Levay."

She let her gaze fall to the Laser, and the rope that tethered it to the dock. It was a clever knot, one of the ones her father taught her. One that held tightly, and looked undoable, but if you gave it a pull in the right direction, it fell apart.

"Get a boat, get to Levay."

Could it be that simple? Just a new approach, with someone to support her, and the whole thing could come loose? If Ajay understood about her father, then maybe other people would too. She'd only really tried talking to him, her mum, Tisha, and Rupert.

A chill spread through her.

Rupert, how could she have forgotten? Rupert could hurt himself. She couldn't bear another memory like the one she already carried. And there was the photo still. There would always be the photo. The internet never forgets. It was all too complicated, too much to untangle.

Unlike the knot in front of her.

"Get a boat, get to Levay."

She leaned forward and pulled.

# CHAPTER FOURTEEN

**AJAY**

I walked along the boardwalk, past the beach huts and shuttered ice cream places. I'd dropped off a resume at the watersports center back in the spring, so I knew exactly where it was: toward the eastern end of town, where the beach curved around to form a semi-sheltered bay.

The guy on the desk was wearing a mask. We silently bonded over it, with a mutual nod as I approached. I doubt I'd have convinced him to loan me a dinghy otherwise. The mask made me look older, for starters. I lied about my age, told him I knew way more about boats than was actually true and signed several forms. Even then, he led me to the smallest, oldest looking boat.

"Back in a couple of hours," I said.

"We close at five." He chucked me a life jacket.

I struggled to untie the rope. For a moment I worried that he'd change his mind and decide I didn't know my knots well enough to borrow the boat, or he'd finally ask for ID. But the guy laughed and came over to help.

"I've been tying things up extra tight lately," he said. "We had a boat drift loose in the summer."

He chucked me the rope, and I caught it, glancing around the old boat, looking for damage. "Not this one?"

He laughed. "Nah, lad. I'm not sending you out in a broken boat, don't worry. Never got the other back. It was a sailboat, just a little Laser."

I nodded, feeling a blank fill itself in. I wasn't sure if Oleander could sail, but she'd grown up by the sea, so it made sense. Maybe she'd decided to "borrow" the Laser to find her own way over to the island?

I gathered up the rope, got in the boat, and set off as quickly as I could, heading straight for the fog bank.

It took me ages to get to the fog. The dinghy was slow, the engine weak. If I looked away, I quickly forgot where I was going, and steered away from the island. I added another note on my hand after the third time: *head for fog*.

Even then, I only kept on course if I stared dead ahead, keeping the fog in my short-term memory. Gulls followed my wobbly path, cawing to each other, as if they were asking themselves what the hell I was trying to do.

I couldn't blame them. I was wondering too.

It was easier to keep on track as I got closer, as the fog filled my vision. I could tell I was getting nearer the island, because every so often the wind brought me snatches of conversation. I tried to listen, but they were too quiet, drowned out by the engine, weak though it was. Tendrils coiled out from the mass of gray toward the boat, reaching toward me, like the tentacles of a hungry sea monster. I shivered.

That wasn't normal for mist, was it?

I checked my phone. It was nearly 3 p.m. I'd have to turn back soon. But the mist seemed closer, nearly there. I couldn't give up, not now. And getting back would be faster. The mainland didn't mess with my head like Levay.

I was at the edge of the mist. A few minutes later, the sea around me grew fuzzier. The gulls stopped wheeling overhead and turned back toward the shore. I wasn't sure if I was no longer interesting, or if they knew something I didn't.

It felt like they were abandoning me.

I kept going, the engine wheezing like my asthmatic aunty, my hand trembling with the shake of the motor. I glanced back at Southcliff. The mist made it fade, dimming its colors and turning it into something unreal.

As the mist swallowed the distant beach completely, the old engine gave a wet splutter, and faded out, leaving me in the silence of the fog.

I pulled on the engine's cord: once, twice, a third time. But the stupid thing wouldn't start. I hit it. That hurt my hand. I swore. A lot.

Even though there was no breeze, a low whispering came from all around me, like the wind and waves were conspiring. The sound grew, hissing around me. I caught snatches of words in different accents.

Perhaps there was another boat, out in the fog like me.

"Hey!" I shouted. "Anyone there?"

I twisted around, trying to focus in the blank gray of the fog, but there was no reply and no other boat. I'd gone so far into the mist I'd lost all sight of the shore.

I pulled on the engine's cord again. It barely spluttered. The waves slapped at the side of the boat.

"Let's get out of here." The whisper felt so close I spun around, expecting to find a girl in the boat with me.

"Are you sure?" a boy answered.

"Come on, behind the manor." Then the sound of running feet, growing distant.

I shivered. It was a trick of the weather conditions. It had to be. Snatches of conversation from the island, brought to me by the strange action of wind and water.

It was a mist, that's all. Nothing more than water vapor.

Seriously creepy water vapor.

Laughter echoed around me, like something from a dinner party. It didn't fit with the mist, with the confusion of the sea. More whispers came, and a baby's cry, jarring and persistent. What kind of an idiot would take a baby out into a fog like this?

The cold of the mist sank deeper, right to my bones. I realized I wasn't even sure which direction Southcliff Beach was anymore.

"Hey?" I shouted again.

The voices continued, and as I stared into the coiling mist, shapes formed. At first, I thought it was just my imagination, trying to make sense of the blank fog. But they grew clearer, ghost-like figures made up of the gray around me: a woman dancing, spinning above the water; a boy rolling down a misty hill; a girl with dark hair, shouting and swearing and falling to the ground as a fist came down on her, again and again and again, until she lay completely still, eyes open, blood seeping from her nose.

I shuffled to the center of the boat.

No. No no no. This did not make sense.

More figures appeared, phantoms in the mist, surrounding

the boat. I held my hands up in pathetically shaking fists to defend myself, but none of the ghosts seemed interested. They carried on like I wasn't even there.

The figures rose and fell, like flames in a fire. A woman in a wedding dress, someone talking to a tour group, crowds in old-fashioned clothes, running at each other with swords and falling to the ground bloodlessly. A man slumped over the steering wheel of a car, in a garage.

I stared at that one until it disappeared, thinking of Oleander.

I pulled out my phone, but there was no reception. I held it up, waving it around, hoping to catch just one weak bar, but it didn't work. I checked the time on it, gone five. Maybe the guy in the watersports center had noticed I wasn't back and would call the coast guard. I slumped back in the boat, feeling like an idiot. I'd gone looking for a forgotten island. Why did I think this would be easy?

I was feeling seasick when she appeared, gliding over the water: a woman in a flowing cloak, hood raised. She moved through the other images, seeming more real than the rest. And while the others ignored me, every so often, she turned to look directly at me. I knew exactly who she was.

The Lady of Levay.

She was beautiful, with a careless ease about her. The sight of her kindled an odd kind of hunger, and I could totally see why Oleander had gone looking for her. Who doesn't have things they want to forget?

She vanished into the mist too quickly for me to see where she went.

I pulled on the engine cord again. Way too many times, until blisters started to form. Eventually I gave up, settled in the middle of the boat as far from the visions as possible and sat there, checking my phone every so often. Still no reception.

The mist grew darker as the evening drew in. No rescue boats appeared.

The visions didn't let up. A birthday cake, with seven bright candles on it; a man digging up weeds in a flowerbed; a girl crawled past, half-submerged, a flash of purple in her wet hair.

I twisted then, trying to see into the mist, trying to follow the specter of Oleander, but she faded into the mass that surrounded me, and I wasn't even sure that it was her.

Is this what had happened to Oleander? Had she died out here, stranded in this madness?

Was she a ghost?

It was about then that I started screaming. I'm not proud of it.

I don't know how long I yelled, but I know it was long enough for my voice to grow hoarse, long enough for me to fade back into silence again.

After that, a horrible numbness crept in, an empty feeling that was worse than the panic. I wondered if that was what a breakdown felt like. How can you tell if you've totally lost it?

Pa and Amma would have got home from Bristol hours ago. They'd be wondering where I was, and why I wasn't answering my phone. At least I'd given the bloke at the watersports center my real name and address, but if the lifeboat people didn't think to look in the fog, they'd never find me.

My notes about Levay were in the bedroom, but I'd told Pa and Amma they were homework, local history. They'd be proud of their dutiful, missing son. Then their minds would slide right off the island again. Maybe they'd stick up posters alongside Sarah.

Just when I'd all but given up hope, the Lady of Levay appeared again.

I scrambled to the side of the boat and called out to her. My hands were shaking, almost numb as I gripped the side. I barely noticed as the boat began to tilt. All my weight was right against the edge as I leaned. Combined with a wave hitting the other side, that's all it took to tip it over. I noticed too late, as the momentum flipped the boat, chucking me out into the sea.

As the cold water covered me, I almost inhaled in shock. I probably would have sunk if it weren't for the life jacket hauling me to the water's surface, where I gulped down air and a mouthful of water and started choking.

A wave slapped me in the face, and another. I doggy-paddled desperately around, looking for my boat, hoping to grab it, to right it, and get back in. But by the time I'd blinked back the sting of the salt water enough to see, the mist had swallowed it and I had no idea which way it had gone.

The sea was cold, sucking the little energy I had left. I shouted, screamed for help, but my voice was weak from my earlier, pointless screaming, and quickly silenced by another mouthful of water.

I had to move. If I stayed where I was the cold would claim me, probably within the hour. If I swam, I might find the boat or get out of the mist.

I had to pick a direction and swim for as long as my body held out.

She appeared again, the woman in gray, coiling out of the mists. Her skirts were submerged in the water ahead of me. She looked back, looked down on me, thrashing in the waves, then walked on, moving elegantly through the other visions.

I got the impression she was leading me somewhere. Maybe it was to death, the ultimate forgetting. But she came from the island, right? She could be returning there, leading me to land.

Southcliff Beach was too far. Levay was my only chance. I didn't have a better plan. I struggled toward her through the waves.

She led me for a long time.

I kicked and gasped until my arms and legs ached, water splashing in my eyes and up my nose. The waves were getting larger. I couldn't tell if the wind was picking up or if we were getting closer to land. I grew weaker. I could no longer keep up with the Lady. She disappeared into the night ahead of me.

Then, so slowly I didn't notice at first, I could see further. I could make out the peaks and troughs of waves a few yards away. The mist was thinning.

I struck out with renewed energy, fighting the growing numbness of my body. The shock of the initial chill had waned, long ago. I didn't feel cold anymore. I felt warm, but there was a growing weight in my hands, in my legs. They no longer felt like a proper part of me.

Then I saw it: the shore.

It was so close, but my strength had almost gone. The ghostly woman stood on the beach, pointing at me. The waves were rough and carried me away to the side, toward sharp rocks that reared out of the rough surf.

The Lady stayed on the beach. I wondered if she was mocking me, if the goddess had let me come this close to safety, knowing I wouldn't be able to make the last bit.

Then I saw someone else, someone real, running down to the water. I tried to shout. The yellow life jacket kept me afloat, but the waves were larger here, breaking as they approached the shore, blinding me, and flinging water down my throat so I could never catch a full breath, could never cry out loud enough.

I was drowning slowly, wave by wave. And I wasn't headed for the shore. The wind, the current pulled me sideways, toward the sharp rocks.

The waves threw themselves on the jagged stones. I was going to be smashed against them. I kicked frantically, thwacked my half-useless arms into the sea, wishing I was fitter, trying to fight the current that dragged me toward the rocks.

I choked and retched on the water forced down my throat. I was getting weaker with each stroke, my lungs filling.

I wasn't going to make it.

# PART TWO

# CHAPTER FOURTEEN

## CHARLOTTE

I ran along the sand. I'd sunk into a perfect rhythm, arms pumping, each step resonating like a second pulse, loud enough to drum the thoughts out of my head. My breath came hard, deep drafts of salty air sucked into my core. All I had to think about was my feet, landing in the wet sand of low tide, kicking up sodden clods as I went.

To my side, the sea was a dark mass under the starless black of the cloudy sky. It hissed at the shore, roiling and wheezing against the pebbles. Mist coiled around the island, drifting like a threat offshore. Most days, Levay Island was surrounded by it: a curtain cutting our small island off from civilization. Its tendrils crept inland at night. Or perhaps that was the wrong way around. Perhaps the mist stole out to sea under cover of darkness, sliding from where it had been hiding among the shadows and secrets of our home during the day.

The moon was already out, and the last of the day's light was just enough to make the wet sand shine. I'd have to turn back soon. The beach ended in a rocky headland at the base of an unstable cliff: a mess of boulders that had tumbled down from the cliff-face in a long-ago landslide. They formed a wall across the beach, marking the furthest point of safety.

I tried not to look at the height of the surviving cliffs beyond. Tried not to imagine what it must have felt like on the day in May when they crumbled beneath my feet, and I fell.

I was lucky I'd survived.

I glanced back over my shoulder at my footsteps, already filled with water: quicksilver pools leading back over the beach, back toward my home, to the fights, the feeling that since the accident I no longer fit in Levay Manor, or on my family's tiny island.

The good thing about running was that I didn't have to think about that. I could forget it all and focus on my pace, on my breath. I could listen to the low mourning of a foghorn far out at sea, and imagine it was some forgotten sea monster, calling out for others of its kind. I listened to whispers in the wind, answering the steady beat of my feet on the shore.

The mist grew thicker ahead of me, between me and the headland, blurring the rocks beyond. It darkened, curled and twisted, and in the twilight, it seemed as if a gray shape swirled up from the ground, like the fog itself was becoming substantial. The hiss of the wind and waves grew around me, building to a rustling murmur.

It looked as if a woman stood in the fog.

She wore a long gray dress. Her legs were shrouded in mist, like knee-deep water.

I tried to stop, stumbling on for a few more steps before coming to a proper halt. I stared at the shape, expecting it to be blown away, to reveal itself for the illusion it was. I leaned my hands on my hot thighs until I caught my breath.

A strange whispering surrounded her, like the muttering of a vast, unseen crowd. She moved. Her head tilted, and I could see her face clearly. It was no trick of the mist.

I was captivated.

The Lady. It was actually the Lady. She was so beautiful, like the stories said, with a face that could cure grief and ease a broken heart; a face that made you feel you could escape your worries, let them go.

We stared at each other for a long moment, silence around us, apart from the inhale and exhale of the sea on the shore and the whisper of the wind.

She turned, pointed to the waves, and faded into nothingness.

"No!" I dashed forward and reached for her, grasping at the mist. She had gone. I swore. Loudly.

It was only then I looked out to the sea, where she had pointed. I almost didn't spot it.

In the near distance, before the mist swallowed the water, something yellow bobbed on the waves. It took me a moment to work out what it was, for the perspective to click into place.

It was a person: someone in a life jacket, tossed on the rough seas.

The tide was pulling him toward the rocks. He didn't have long.

I ran into the water.

# CHAPTER FOURTEEN

## AJAY

I was losing consciousness, well-confused. I couldn't even doggy-paddle, and the stupid waves kept whacking me in the face. I grabbed breaths when I could, but I had no strength. I couldn't see anyone on the shore when I got a glimpse of it. The Lady of Levay and the girl had vanished. If they'd ever been there.

The current hauled me toward the rocks. The waves were high, and they smashed themselves to pieces on the stones. I couldn't fight as they dragged me closer, ready to do the same to me.

I thought she was a hallucination for a second, yet another bloody vision from the mist. Then for a wild moment I thought she was Oleander, come to rescue me.

I only realized she was real when I felt her arm around my chest. I looked down and saw it, pale and solid, holding tightly to me, through the blur of my salt-stained vision. She was pulling me away from the breaking waves, from the sharp stones. She was swimming us both toward shore, but not very well.

She swore and choked on a mouthful of seawater. I tried to look at her, but I couldn't bend my neck enough. I caught a glance of a bob of brown hair plastered against her cheek. Dark hair over dark waves. Her swearing made me feel better. It made her real, unmysterious. It was so good to have an actual human there after the madness of the mist.

I looked toward the shore and a horrible fact became obvious. We weren't going to make it to the beach.

The tide was pulling us away, and although the girl fought it, she wasn't strong enough to get us around the headland.

She swore under her breath again, words censored by a wave that hit us both. She changed direction, giving up on the cove to prevent us being smashed on the rocks. She steered us parallel to the shore. She was struggling too, coughing in my ear, spluttering out seawater. The tide dragged us toward the bottom of the cliffs where the waves broke in booming explosions of foam. Just when I thought we were going to be thrown against the cliff, a black gash opened in the rock wall. The waves carried us right to it and hurled us into the dark.

It was a cave.

The water swirled around the entrance, sucking us into the darkness. The girl swam with the current, guiding us to one side, deeper in until it was almost pitch black. When she let me go, I panicked for a moment but felt ground under my kicking feet. The girl tugged on my life jacket and helped me heave my torso out of the water and onto a flat rock at the side of the cave.

I lay on my side as we both gasped for air. I could barely make her out; she was just a dark shape in the nearly pitch-black cave, coughing, retching, choking up seawater. My life jacket propped me up at an awkward angle. I couldn't feel the rocks beneath me. They were just pressure on my numb skin. I was coughing too, and when I could finally speak, my voice was weak.

"Thanks."

"We're not safe." She sounded hoarse too, her accent posh. She coughed again, a gross, wet sound, hacking up sea water. "This cave fills at high tide. We have to get out and back around to the cove."

"I don't think I can make it."

"You have to." I felt her hand around my arm, a touch of warmth. "We'll rest for a moment, then go. I'll help."

I could see it then, her struggling to drag me through the waves, a dead weight, dooming us both.

I wasn't going to be responsible for another death.

"No. Take the life jacket." I tried to wriggle out of the bloody thing, tried to undo the clasp, but my fingers didn't work properly. "Save yourself."

"I'm not leaving you!" Her plummy tone was as outraged as if I'd suggested a disgusting sex act. I liked her then. She coughed some more.

"Take the life jacket and get help, then," I said.

She was silent for a moment, considering this. "My father has a boat," she croaked, finally. "Our house isn't far. We might have time."

She must have been part of the family that owned the island, then. It made sense. Who else would be here?

"Help me get this thing off."

I guided her hands in the dark, and she unclasped and unzipped the life jacket. It clung to my wet clothes, but we got it off. I heard her zip it up on herself.

"Move back," she said. "The cave rises that way. It'll buy you some time."

"Good luck." I wanted to say goodbye.

"I'll be back soon."

There was a splash as she jumped into the water, and the horrible sense of her absence in the dark. I sat there catching my breath for what felt like a long time before I realized the waves were lapping around my back. The water was rising.

I did what she'd told me, shuffling toward the back of the cave, pulling myself over flatter rocks, crawling over the more jagged ones, feeling ahead with my hands in the pitch black.

I ached all over. It was hard going. I was way more tired than I should be. When I reached some almost-dry rocks, I fought the urge to lie down. I had to keep going.

The cave went further back than I'd thought. It took a while to reach the end of it. The boom of the waves against the cliff outside got quieter. I strained my eyes but couldn't see a bloody thing. Eventually, the wall rounded. I followed it with my hands. I'd found the back.

Now what?

Would I die here? I thought of my parents, wondering where I was, and felt like I was going to vomit. They'd never know what happened to me.

Is this what had happened to Oleander? Had Levay claimed her life?

Levay. I turned the word over in my head. Levay. I remembered the name.

I couldn't see the notes on my hands in dark. They'd probably been washed away, but I didn't seem to need them. Now I'd reached the island itself, I could remember it. It made an odd kind of sense. How could you forget an island when you were on it?

This whole thing was so weird.

I pushed my back against the damp cave wall. My sleepiness grew. I slapped myself in the face, hard. It woke me up a little but not enough.

"Hello!"

The voice echoed through the cave, and for a moment, I thought it might be the hallucinations. It was too soon. There was no way she could have got a boat and got back already.

"Hello?" The girl cried out, and it was for sure her, posh croaky voice and everything.

"Here!" I put all I had into that shout. "I'm here!"

"Where are you?"

"Back of the cave!"

"Keep talking."

I did, yammering stupidly about where I was, over and over again. Then I felt her, in the darkness. A hand brushed against my shoulder and followed my arm down. I felt the warmth of her skin on my fingers, and in that moment, no touch had ever felt so good.

"You're so cold," she said, and her voice was way too sad.

I felt like I was standing on the edge of a hole. "The ... boat. You got the boat?"

Silence, for a few seconds.

"I'm so sorry. The current's too strong. I couldn't get around the headland. The sea washed me back into the cave. I tried, again and again, but the last time, I ... couldn't find the way out. The mouth of the cave is underwater." She squeezed my hand tighter.

"We're trapped here."

# CHAPTER FIFTEEN

## CHARLOTTE

The dark felt tight around us as the water rose. The boy was weak. His skin was too cold. He was probably hypothermic. I wondered if there was a way I could warm him up, then realized that was silly.

We would both drown long before he died of cold.

"I'm sorry," I said.

His hand was slightly bigger than mine, and it was comforting to hold it. I wished I could see him.

"I'm the one who fell in the sea. Total idiot. This is so my fault."

He had a nice voice, softly deep with a London accent. I squeezed his hand, glad he'd said that. As I'd fought the waves, fought to escape the cave and the sucking current, all I could think was that I let him down.

"It's not your fault," I said.

He squeezed my hand back.

Cold water swirled around my calves. My feet were growing numb. Although I couldn't see anything, I imagined the sea as a deeper darkness, liquid black. It felt as if I wouldn't so much drown as dissolve into its oily depths. I leaned against the wet cave wall for balance.

I thought of my parents, of all I'd put them through when I'd gone missing before. Now they'd lose me for good. They might never know what happened. They'd worked so hard to make me better, and I'd thrown it all away.

As the water rose, the air around me felt thicker, wetter.

Moisture came with each breath. I moved closer to the boy, and it was good to be near him. To feel the length of his arm against mine and my hand in his. To feel the in and out of his breath next to me.

"I'm Charlotte, by the way."

"Ajay. Nice to meet you."

He pumped my hand, a parody of a formal shake. We both started laughing at the ridiculousness of it all, and the cave felt a little less cold, a little less dark.

At least I wouldn't be dying alone.

As the tide pushed the water up to thigh-height, the edge of a sound cut through the dark: soft, but clearly not waves, not wind. I focused, trying to work out where it had come from in the featureless dark, tilting my head to try to hear it.

It came again: a voice, then another.

They were a little way in front of me, muffled by the muted roar of the tide at the mouth of the cave, but getting clearer as they got closer. I didn't catch what they said, but my heart leapt. Maybe one of my parents saw us swept into the cave. Maybe they'd got divers in to help.

"There's someone there!" I said. "Hey! We're here! Help!"

A second voice joined the first. They spoke to each other in the dark not far away, words swallowed by the hiss of water as each wave pushed the sea further into the cave.

"We're here!" Ajay yelled. "At the back!"

They didn't respond.

The first voice sounded young, almost a boy, and the second was an older man. I couldn't understand a word they were saying. Perhaps they were foreign. It didn't matter. Someone was here. Someone had found us.

"Hey!"

"We're here! The back of the cave."

They kept talking to each other and showed no sign of having heard us.

"Why don't they have lights?" Ajay asked. "Wouldn't a rescue team have lights?"

He was right. Fear dropped into my stomach like a stone.

When Ajay spoke again there was a bitter twist in his voice. "They're not real, are they? They're hallucinations."

"But I can hear them," I said. "We can both hear them, right?"

The voices continued their conversation. The boy sounded panicked, but the younger man spoke soothingly, almost coaxing the boy. Then came the rustle of clothing, a grunt of effort, then the scrape of a boot or a shoe, on the wall to my left, but higher up.

The boy's voice came from in front of me again, sounding surprised. It was answered by the laughter of the older man from high up the stony wall at the back, and a sentence where the tone of the voice communicated "I told you so" as clearly as if he were speaking English.

"Can you understand them?" Ajay asked.

"No. But it sounds like one of them is above us."

There were more grunts, more scrambling, and I could hear the boy scuffling against the back wall. There were a few moments of panting, followed by the boy's voice above us, along with backslapping and laughter. After that, the two voices grew fainter. I couldn't tell if they were growing more distant, or just fading out, leaving us back in reality, in the dark, rising sea, on our own.

The water was up to my waist. It sloshed around, less violent than the full force of the waves outside but threatening the delicate grip I had on my own balance. I couldn't let myself be swept off my feet, be dragged into the cold.

Something touched my leg. I fumbled in the dark, trying not to scream, and my fingers caught on the wet tangle of seaweed wrapping itself around my knee. I hurled it away from me, then tried to breathe normally, tried to get hold of myself.

"Are you okay?" Ajay asked.

"Yeah, just seaweed."

"Where did the voices go?"

"I don't know. But we should look and find out."

"Is that a good idea?"

"The only other plan I have is 'give up and drown.'"

Ajay paused, as if considering this. "Then I'm all in on the 'follow the hallucinations' idea."

I thought it best not to mention that was what had got me into this situation.

I turned to the sheer stone wall behind us. It was slippery, and as I ran a hand over it, it seemed damper than it should be from just the sea spray. I kept my hand in place for a few seconds, and the wet trickled over my fingers. It was coming down the wall, from somewhere above.

The water would make it harder to climb, but it had to be coming from somewhere. I reached up, grabbed a rock, and tried to find a place to put my shoe. It was pathetic. I slid down immediately and landed with a splash in the water.

"Can you climb?" I asked Ajay.

"I can barely feel my hands."

Again I tried. This time I managed to get my second foot up onto a handy rock on the wall, but it just made my fall worse when my grip failed and I fell backward, splashing down into the sea. Water rushed up my nose, stinging and making me cough and splutter.

I tried a few more times, with even less success. I wanted to take off my shoes, but it was hard to lift my foot up out and keep my balance, and my fingers were too numb to work the laces.

Then I had my best, most dangerous idea yet.

I couldn't climb and neither could Ajay. We'd probably both been in the water too long. But sooner or later, we wouldn't have to climb. I may not have the strength in my arms to heave myself up the wall, but I had something more powerful.

I had the sea.

I just had to not drown for long enough that the water lifted me up to where the voices had disappeared.

Easier said than done. The longer we spent in the cold water, the worse our odds were, especially for Ajay. As the water rose, inch by inch, it sucked the energy from me, leeching my warmth.

I took the life jacket off and put it back on Ajay, even though he protested.

"Let the water take your weight," I said. "Keep hold of the wall."

I grabbed a couple of hand-holds and let the water buoy me up. The tide tugged at me, tried to pull me from my perch, but I didn't have to hold my whole weight, the water was doing that for me.

"Are you still there?" I said.

"Yes." Ajay's voice was weak.

As the water rose, I climbed. It was tough. I had to cling to the wall and kick my feet to keep afloat as the water pushed me up it. I was long past shivering. But I was higher than I'd been able to reach before. The wall sloped backward here, no longer going straight up. I was able to lean my weight against it, rather than hanging off the sheer wall. Hand over hand, I pulled myself up and out of the sea, scraping my stomach against the rough surface.

I reached above, to where I'd assumed the roof of the cave would be. There was a moment of crushing disappointment as my fingers touched the rock directly overhead. I couldn't feel the detail of it; just the pressure against my nearly-dead fingers. But as I dragged them along, the pressure vanished. I waved my hand into the gap I'd found, the hole in the cave's ceiling, above and ahead of me. It wasn't wide, maybe a couple of feet. The ground there was wet, water seeping out and trickling down the wall.

It would have been impossible to find that space at the back of the cave without following the voices. But it was there.

"I … I think there's a gap here."

"A way out?" Ajay asked.

"I don't know."

I wiggled up further, beached-whale style. I grunted and dragged myself until my head and shoulders were in the gap. It levelled out, and I was able to get my whole body in.

I reached into the pitch-black space. My finger-tips touched nothing ahead, but the walls were still there on either side. The space was high enough for me to move into a crouch, and turn around to face toward Ajay, but I banged my head on the ceiling as I did so, the blow reverberating through my skull and jaw.

"Ow!"

"What happened? You okay?"

"Yes. Just bumped my head. There's room for both of us up here."

"Will the tide get up there?"

"I don't know. I think we can move further back. I'll pull you up."

I reached down, swinging my arms into the blackness below until I hit his head.

"Sorry."

I waved in the dark again, and this time found his hand, reached up toward me. We fumbled at each other until I had his other hand too.

"Ready? One, two, three."

I pulled and he kicked at the water. I worried my wet hands would slip from his as I heaved him higher, over the sloping wall. Together, my muscles screaming, we got the dead weight of him up and into the gap.

"Right," I said, once we'd both caught our breath. "Let's see how far back this thing goes."

# CHAPTER SIXTEEN

## AJAY

I could hear Charlotte crawling ahead of me in the pitch black. It was hard to keep up, but I kept going, just about, and so did the tunnel.

It was wet, but there were only a couple of inches of water to crawl through, more like a slow-moving puddle than a proper stream. It was a bit of a stretch to call it a "tunnel," really. It was a horizontal crack in the ground, probably hollowed out by the water that ran through it. Just big enough to shuffle ahead commando-style, on my forearms.

I was no commando at the best of times.

I was shaking way too hard. I wished I could see something, wished I didn't have to grope around me to keep from hitting my head while still trying to shuffle forward.

The tunnel took us back and upward.

"We have awesome hallucinations," I said, and Charlotte laughed. But my tongue felt heavy in my mouth as I spoke, and I'd sounded drunk.

That was not good, especially as I had many questions. They'd have to wait until we got wherever the tunnel was leading us.

I scraped my arms and knees, but the pain helped to keep me awake as the sleepiness threatened to take me.

"It's higher here!" Charlotte called out from ahead of me. "You can crawl."

"Nice!" But when I tried to push myself up, I didn't have the strength to get onto my hands and knees. I was pathetically weak.

"We're okay!" Charlotte shouted, a little while later. Her voice was distant. She was way further ahead than I'd expected. "There's a bigger cave here! We'll be safe until the tide goes out again."

Her words got messed up in my head. I didn't get what she was saying. I lay my head on the stone. I knew it was cold, but I felt warm. It felt like the fog had got into my brain, like it was muffling my senses. I wished I could see what Charlotte looked like. I liked her laugh. I wasn't into posh girls, but she sounded okay. Maybe it was the seawater croak in her voice. It took the edge off all that class crap and made her sound like a forty-a-day smoker.

The ground felt so comfy, better than any pillow. I wondered if I'd closed my eyes or not. I couldn't tell.

My thoughts got all weird then, and Charlotte and Oleander merged. It made a kind of sense. I'd followed Oleander to the island; I'd followed Charlotte into the tunnels.

Or perhaps she was a hallucination, too.

Maybe I'd followed in Oleander's footsteps, all the way to the end. Perhaps she had washed up here and died in the cave, or maybe she'd made it as far as I had, deep into this tunnel, following hallucinations in the dark. For some reason, the idea of her dying didn't seem so bad since I wasn't going to make it either.

I could forget about everything I'd done wrong. Making Meera sick. Letting Oleander down. I could forget it all.

Perhaps when I died, I'd get to see them both again.

# CHAPTER SEVENTEEN

## CHARLOTTE

I'd lost all sense of direction. I waved my arms in the darkness ahead of me and felt nothing. I reached up, standing on tiptoes, and couldn't touch the ceiling. I walked forward, but the water got deeper, up to my ankles.

Maybe I was close to home. Maybe this was the groundwater my father was always saying was too high, seeping into the basement of our house.

There was no light and no breeze, so no way out. It didn't matter. There was no way the tide could rise high enough to drown us here. Elation warmed me, even in my wet clothes.

"We're okay!" I called back to Ajay. "There's a bigger cave here! We'll be safe until the tide goes out again."

I walked forward, out of the water, hands groping, reaching into the darkness. My foot hit something, which rolled away with a low noise that made me think of stone.

Curious, I let my hands lead me down to the ground. On the floor there were pieces of rock. I stuck one of them in my pocket. I could find out what they were later. Because there was going to be a later. We just had to wait for low tide, then the water would be shallow enough for us to get out around the headland. We could see the sky again.

I noticed how quiet the space was.

"Ajay?"

No answer.

"Ajay!"

That was when I felt the full force of my blindness. It wasn't so bad when he was with me, but now I was alone in the dark.

"Ajay! Where are you?"

Something had happened to Ajay. Something in the dark.

I turned, trying to remember which way the tunnel was. I stumbled forward, hands out, fighting the urge to cry.

I tripped over something, and landed on my hands and knees, grazing them. My breath came in shaky gasps and I crawled forward, awkwardly. My hand touched something, and I recoiled, only to realize it was the wall. My hands were wet, water trickling over my knuckles. At least I'd found the stream again.

That was good. I could follow the stream back. I focused on the soft movement of the water against my fingertips, then followed the flow.

"Ajay!" The utter black felt tight around me, making it hard to breathe as I crawled. I hadn't got far before my fingers encountered something softer, more yielding than rock, and warmer.

A body. Ajay's body.

"Ajay!" I grabbed his arm and shook. He didn't respond. He was on his side, mostly out of the water. I followed the arm up to his neck, intending to check his pulse, but I could feel the in and out of breath in his chest. He still wore the life jacket, even though it must have made it difficult for him to crawl.

"Ajay?"

"Hmm?" He sounded like I'd woken him.

"Are you okay?"

"Mmm."

He trembled under my hands. How long had he been in the water when I saw him? There'd been no boat in sight.

He was hypothermic. That mattered now we weren't going to drown. He needed warmth. It wasn't too cold in the cave, I realized. It was a lot warmer than outside and sheltered from the wind. But I needed to get him out of the stream he still partly lay in.

It wasn't easy. He was a total dead weight, and there wasn't much room for maneuver in the tunnel. In the end, I pulled him along by the life jacket as I crawled. I worried that I was grazing and bruising him against the rough floor and walls, but I guessed it wouldn't matter. Bruises and scrapes were the least of his worries.

I reached the cave, and stood up, dragging him out of the stream. I cracked my hip against the wall and yelled in pain, my own voice reflecting back to me from the unseen walls. Once the flare of hot hurt calmed, I shouted deliberately and listened. The room wasn't loud enough for a distant echo, but it wasn't small either. I guessed it was about the size of a church.

I got down on my hands and knees. Ajay's clothes were soaking. I unzipped his life jacket, and got it off him. I tugged at his wet jumper, but it clung to his chest. You were meant to get hypothermic people out of their wet clothes. But what were you meant to do when there were no dry clothes to put them in? Let them lie naked on the cold stone? That didn't sound right.

I'd read an old romance of my mother's, back when I'd been in the early stages of recovery and desperate for entertainment.

In it, a woman was hypothermic after an avalanche and the hot rich man got her back to his tent and they spooned naked in his sleeping bag, so he could use his body warmth to save her. But I had no sleeping bag, and I wasn't even sure if that was a real thing, or a flimsy plot device to get them into a sexy situation.

If he did wake up, Ajay probably wouldn't take too kindly to finding I'd stripped him naked and was spooning him while he was unconscious.

I'd have to do my best with my body warmth through our clothes and my breath. I laid out the life jacket on the ground, then rolled him onto it, to keep him off the cold rock. I lay behind him and hugged him, pressing as much of me against him as I could, to share the little warmth I had with him.

I was glad he was unconscious, as I felt totally awkward doing it.

He shivered. Even though he was taller than me, bigger than me in every way, he felt fragile.

How long would it take for the tide to go back out? I didn't have a watch, but if I concentrated, I could hear the muted boom and hiss of the sea at a distance, down the tunnel. Perhaps I would be able to hear when it had gone.

Sometimes Ajay made slight noises. He sounded confused, muttering and mumbling. I caught odd words, a name that he whispered a few times, and shouted once: Oleander. I wondered who she was. I wondered who he was, this strange boy who had washed up at my island without a boat.

Why had he gone out in such an impenetrable mist?

After a while, the distant heave and roil of the sea began to match with my breath on Ajay's neck. In and out, my breath and the waves. In and out, a calm and steady rhythm laid over the shaking of our bodies. Ajay's breathing was shallower, faster than mine, but there was warmth between us. The front of my shirt and the back of his jumper felt cozy. I clutched him tighter, for my own comfort as much as his, as I breathed my warmth into the space between us, in and out, until sleep came.

A shout woke me.

I sat up. Cold air rushed between Ajay and me. I desperately tried to open my eyes, thinking I was stuck in the darkness of sleep, until I realized my eyes were open. There was nothing to see.

Ajay stirred. He shivered still, but his breaths were slower, longer, and deeper.

My body was stiff from the cold and aching with pulled muscles. I twisted this way and that as I tried to listen, tried to hear where the shout had come from. But there was no sound in the cave other than the two of us. It must have been my dream, or another hallucination.

It took me a moment to realize the other significance of the silence.

I couldn't hear the sea. The soft boom of the waves no longer reached us from the tunnel.

"Ajay," I said, shaking him. "Ajay."

"Hmm?"

"I think the tide might have gone out. We have to get out of here."

"Let me ... hang on." His voice sounded thick with sleep still, but it was stronger.

"I'll go," I said. "See if the tide really is out. If you can't move, I'll get help."

"I can move. Just give me a minute."

"Try to stay warm," I said, then realized how pointless that was. "I'll be quick."

It wasn't easy to crawl back through the tunnel. My body was bruised and battered, and twinges of pain hit me with almost every movement. When I reached the opening of the tunnel, I still couldn't see a thing. The sound of the sea came at a distance, and there was no swirling of water below me.

Even if the tide wasn't fully out, it might still be shallow enough to wade around the headland. It was our best shot. I doubted Ajay would survive if we waited much longer, and the tide could be coming in again.

I turned, careful not to hit my head in the low space as I shuffled back to get Ajay. I'd got about three quarters of the way when I heard a noise ahead of me in the dark.

"Ajay?"

"I've brought the life jacket."

"Good." I hadn't realized how worried I was until the relief flooded me.

We really were going to make it.

# CHAPTER EIGHTEEN

## AJAY

I tried to keep up with Charlotte. Everything was hard. My body shook. My arms and legs could hardly hold me. I clutched the life jacket as I crawled. I'd wanted to put it on, but my fingers wouldn't work properly. Now they were locked around the jacket's strap. I crawled on the knuckles of that hand. They were probably bleeding, but I couldn't feel it. Still, I tried to keep my weight off that side.

The darkness was getting to me. Blackness lurked at the corners of my mind. The mist filled my head. I had so many questions for Charlotte, but I couldn't think. I crawled instead. When the tunnel lowered, I wriggled on like a worm.

"Ajay, we're at the cave." Charlotte's posh voice was slightly less hoarse, and it sounded reassuringly familiar, after all we'd been through. "I'm going to lower you down. Try to hold on to the wall, okay?"

She eased the life jacket out of my frozen hand, uncurling my fingers, and she dropped it down ahead of us. She helped me turn around and clutched my arms as she lowered me, feet first, down into the cave. I was glad it was pitch black. It was humiliating enough as it was.

I struggled to find foot holds but only found empty air. I kicked at the wall, slipped from Charlotte's hands and fell the rest of the way, scraping my chin.

The life jacket broke my fall, but the pain was intense in my arms, shoulder, and chin. I'd also bent one leg an awkward way, and my knee screamed at me.

"Are you okay?" Charlotte sounded breathless above me.

"I … yeah. I think." That was crap. I wasn't sure if I could walk on my bad leg.

"Can you move out of the way? I'm coming down."

I rolled my protesting body off to one side and heard her scramble and scrape down the rock. She landed more elegantly than I had. Her hands groped for me in the dark, touching my hair, then my shoulder.

"Let's go."

I tried to stand. My knee exploded in agony as I attempted to put weight on it. I half-screamed, embarrassingly, and collapsed again.

"Sorry. It's my knee. I landed on it."

"Which knee?"

"The left side."

I felt her grope around me, until she was on my left. She lifted my arm and put her shoulder up under it.

"One, two, three."

I stood, just about. Most of my weight was on her. We stumbled like that through the darkness of the cave. There was no water now, but the wet ground was uneven, and we moved slowly with me virtually hopping. I could feel her trying to push me on, gently, obviously thinking about the tide.

The wind blew into the cave. I wouldn't've thought I could get colder, but I did. My clothes were still damp, and the breeze chilled them.

I thought I might be passing out as a dark gray patch grew in the center of my vision. Then it clicked into place.

"I … I can see the way out."

"I know." Her voice was filled with such relief I fought tears welling up in my eyes. I was glad she couldn't see me.

The gray in front of us grew bigger, but not brighter. It was only when we reached the mouth of the cave that I got why.

It was the middle of the night. A cloudy night, the stars and moon hidden. But I was still totally happy to see it. The sea lapped at the shore, tame and soft. Not like the vicious waves that had carried us into the cave.

There was a headland to our right that reached out into the sea: the rocks I'd almost been thrown against. There was no chance I could climb over them in the state I was in.

"We timed it perfectly," Charlotte said. "This is as low as it gets. But we'll still have to wade a little. Put this on."

Her face was in darkness as she held out the life jacket. I tried to put it on but was totally rubbish at it. She sat me down and between the two of us, we did it. She put her shoulder under my arm again and we stumbled down into the sea.

I didn't brace myself for the cold. I was so bloody freezing I didn't expect the water to make any difference. But it did.

Charlotte must have felt it too, as she moved closer to me, her arm around my back. She pulled me in to her. I felt stupidly grateful to have her close as the water tugged at our feet.

We waded deeper, and although it took the weight off my bad leg, it was hard to keep my balance as the water rose up above my waist. I looked at her, but she had turned away from me, focusing on the coast. I could just make out the dark bob of her wet hair. I wondered what she looked like.

"Just float," she said as we got chest-deep. "I've got this."

I wanted to protest, but it would have been macho crap that could put us both in danger. I let the waves take my weight. I could see how much easier it made it for her, as she held the loop on the back of the life jacket. She still struggled, but she could pull me, and no longer had to balance the two of us against the sea. Waves slapped in my face, blinding me.

It didn't take long to get around the headland. She went ahead, dragging me to the shore. As it got too shallow for her to pull, I crawled up, past the strings of seaweed to the dry rocks, clear of the sea's reach, with the last of my energy.

"I'm going to get help. I won't be long. Stay here, okay?"

"Do I have to?" I said as I collapsed onto my front, face against the stones, blinking to clear my eyes of the sting of salt.

She paused, then got that I was joking. She started laughing. I felt her lean over, and kiss the back of my head quickly, an excited, thoughtless kiss.

"We made it," she said, softly into my ear.

Then she was gone, running up the beach. I managed to pull myself up enough to watch her run, a shape in the dark.

I rolled over and stared at the starless sky.

For better or worse, I'd made it to Levay.

Had Oleander?

# CHAPTER NINETEEN

## CHARLOTTE

I ran up the beach. My legs were weak and I stumbled over stones. I sprawled onto the shingle, grazing my knees and hands, then scrambled to my feet and kept running. I was glad I hadn't been able to take my shoes off in the cave, or I'd be limping on the stony ground. But they were soaking wet. Each footstep felt like I was squelching further into them.

I had to get home. Had to get help for Ajay.

I sprinted to the path that led from the beach up the hill toward the manor. The grass was dark and high on either side, and it whispered around me. I was breathless as I saw the manor: a black silhouette against the night sky, windows dark.

A light bobbed in the grounds to my right. I froze, thinking of ghosts, hallucinations, and the Lady of Levay. But the light was too bright, too normal. It grew brighter, focusing on me, catching in my eyes and blinding me.

"Charlotte!" My father's voice, frantic. "Charlotte!"

The light dropped down then, pointing at the ground. It bounced as he ran, rustling through the long grass toward me.

"Charlotte! I've been looking for you for hours." He looked

furious, but as he approached, and saw me properly, the anger was replaced with confusion.

"You're soaking. What happened?"

"I ..." At the sight of him, whatever had been holding me together dissolved. I collapsed on my knees. He rushed over and swooped me up in a hug, and I tried to talk as the emotion rushed through me, swallowing my words in breathless, uncontrollable sobs.

He put his arm around my back, providing support, and hurried me toward the house. "You're so cold, Charlotte. We have to get you inside."

It felt good to be helped, good to be taken care of after all those hours trying to keep Ajay alive.

"Help Ajay, please. He's on the beach."

I knew my father could barely hear me. My voice was hoarse from the salt water, and my breath jolted out of me in gasps as he steered me home.

"How long were you in the water? What happened?"

We were almost at the house. I shook my head. "He's on the shore. Have to get him here. Have to get him warm."

"Get who warm? Charlotte, you're not making sense." Irritation was seeping into his voice. I had to get hold of myself. For Ajay's sake.

We were at the main door. My father half supported, half-carried me in. I tried to breathe, tried to calm down.

"There was a boy in the water. I went in to save him." I had to stop and swallow my tears. "He's on the shore. Help him. Please."

My father's eyes widened. "There's a boy on the shore?"

I nodded. He glanced into the dark, toward the beach, clearly torn. "How? Are you sure?"

"Yes. Absolutely."

"But you need help now. You're so cold."

My tears threatened to choke me. "He's worse. Please."

"One second." He ran into the house.

I stood there, dripping on the marble of the grand entrance hall, knowing there wasn't time for whatever he was doing. But he was back in a few seconds, carrying what looked like towels.

"Here," he handed one to me, and I could see it was a bathrobe. "Get out of those wet clothes. Put this on. Run a hot bath and get in it. Now. I'll look after the boy."

He sprinted out of the house, clutching the other bathrobe.

I woke in my bed, feeling like I'd just come out of an intense dream I couldn't remember. My sheets were soft, but bruises and grazes ached all over my body.

I stared at the wall for a long moment. There was a lengthening crack there. It had grown even in the last few days. I stared at it, exhausted. I turned over to go back to sleep and felt the flare of pain as I discovered new cuts and tender spots. They woke me properly, and I sat up, staring at my four-poster, at my room, remembering the events of the night before: the cave, Ajay.

I must have fallen asleep, that was obvious. I remembered shampooing salt and seaweed out of my hair. I stayed in just long enough that I felt warm again. I knew Ajay would need time to get out of his clothes, and whether he needed Dad's help or not, he definitely wouldn't appreciate me being there. So once I'd pulled on some warm pajamas, I took the time to dry and straighten my hair. Had I gone right to bed after that? It wasn't unusual to forget going to bed. Just like you forget getting dressed most days.

But wouldn't I have gone to check on Ajay?

I'd been losing time since the accident. Had that happened again? I glanced at the clock on my bedside table. It was five a.m. I had no idea what time I'd got home from the cave or how long I'd been in bed.

I swung my feet out of bed. My muscles protested as I stood, aches right through my body. I pulled the pajama shirt down at my shoulder, and the bruise there was red and purple, fresh and vivid.

I crept into the hall. Voices came from down the passage, and I headed for those, although as I approached their bedroom door, I realized I couldn't hear Ajay, just my mother and father. I was about to go in and ask where he was, when I caught my name. I didn't hear what my mother was saying about me, just my father's reply.

"She's still recovering, Eleanor. Give her time."

"How much time, Peter? We need to reopen the house. We're still paying off the debt from the pandemic. We need to bring in more money."

"You don't need to worry."

As if to prove him wrong, the lights faded, then flickered back to full brightness.

He sighed. "That was just the generator. You know how it can be."

"We're running off the generator? What's wrong with the mains?"

"I think we got cut off. I'll look into it, okay?" He sounded frustrated.

"You do that. And there are new cracks appearing. We need to get the engineers in."

"The house has held together for centuries. It'll be fine for a couple more weeks. Things are nearly back to normal."

"You keep saying that."

"Because it's true."

"It's not." The door was open a crack. I put my eye to it. I couldn't see my father from where I stood, just my mother. She swayed a little as she spoke, perhaps still tipsy from the gin I'd seen her knocking back last night. Typical. "What's she doing running out into the sea on a night like this? I mean yes, she saved the boy, but she should have come here and got us."

At least that had to mean Ajay was safe in the house somewhere.

"What was she thinking? She's so reckless now."

I leaned back. As far as my mother was concerned, I couldn't do anything right.

"There were problems before the accident too," my father said.

"At least she spoke properly then. She even carried herself well. Look at her now."

"She's getting better. She's been working hard on her exercises and elocution."

I winced at that. I had been a bit half-hearted lately.

"She's still clumsy, and she used to be so graceful. What if she doesn't recover more? What if she's always like this?"

Daddy's jaw clenched. "You worry too much."

"She's been biting her nails, and she used to take such care of them."

I ran my hand over my hair, feeling self-conscious. I'd straightened my bob, but the sea air was already making it frizz. Yes, I'd started biting my nails. And there hadn't seemed much point in putting on varnish, not when there was just the three of us here.

"She should be back at school. Obviously not St. Catherine's. They were no good at all. We should try to get her into Roedean. Maybe they'd have some sympathy. They should understand about cliffs, at least, considering their grounds."

Daddy spoke through gritted teeth. "Stop it. Charlotte is fine. You have no patience."

I hadn't seen him that frustrated before. It wasn't like him. While it was nice to hear him defending me, there was something about his voice that made me uneasy.

My mother took a deep breath and replied in a conciliatory tone. "I've had patience, Peter. I've tried. Really, I have. But she's not fine. Maybe it was all that time in the water. Maybe it was the injuries."

My breath caught in my throat, but she kept talking.

"I think there was permanent damage done. There's something wrong with Charlotte."

It was a gut-punch to hear the words coming out of my mother's mouth. I stepped back from the door, wishing I could unhear it. I closed my eyes, and breathed deeply. It was one thing to suspect you weren't okay, it was another to hear your mother confirm it.

I swallowed, trying to pull myself together. I didn't want my parents to catch me out here, didn't want them to know I'd overheard. And I needed to find Ajay. He had to be in the house somewhere, but I wasn't going to ask my parents where they'd put him now.

I tried to put the conversation out of my mind and focus. Where would he be?

As I stood, thinking, I noticed the smell of woodsmoke. Ajay needed warmth, so it made sense that my father would have lit a fire for him. I followed the smell down the hall to the Red Room, the smallest bedroom, the room my father sometimes slept in when he was fighting with my mother.

I eased the door open. There was a lump under the blanket, a dark head protruding, and I exhaled.

It took me a few seconds to realize Ajay wasn't alone.

In the darkest corner, furthest from the fireplace, something moved. Something misty. It twisted, as if with the breeze. But there was no breeze in the room.

The Lady of Levay.

Cold clutched at my chest.

She stood by the bed, in the shadows. Ajay's head was on the pillow, only his dark hair visible from where I stood, his face toward her. Something was rising from him, something that coiled and rose like steam. Images swirled in the mist that flowed toward her. I couldn't quite make them out, but one of the pictures in the fog was my face.

"What —"

I didn't get any further. The Lady looked at me, panic in her beautiful eyes.

She dissipated, fading into the mist around her until she was gone.

I rushed to Ajay's side, and laid a hand on him. What had she been taking from him? His breath? His soul? His life?

The red blanket rose and fell at his chest. He wasn't dead. He was sleeping deeply, by the look of it. Maybe I'd got there just in time.

An arm was thrown on top of the blanket, wearing the tartan of one of Daddy's thick flannel pajama shirts. The fire was down to its embers, but it still warmed the room.

The windows were leaded with a diamond pattern and looked out toward the sea. I peered through them, but there was no sign of the woman out there, just Levay's ever-present mist in the early morning darkness.

Ajay needed to sleep, needed to recover. But what if the woman came back? I'd protected him in the caves, and I'd got him safely home. I wasn't going to lose him here.

I crept to the side of the bed, and looked down at him for the first time, properly. I'd barely seen him in the water, blinded as I was by sea-spray, and in the cave, it had been too dark to see anything.

He lay on the pillow, a peaceful expression on his slumbering face. There was a Band-aid above one bushy eyebrow, too pale on his dark skin. His thick hair was crusty with salt. I fought back an urge to touch it, to run my hand through it. I imagined how it would feel, the softness under the stiff.

I had to admit, he was cute, sleeping, and I wondered if he looked that good when he was awake. As if offended by my train of thought, he gave a sleep snort and turned over.

I had a lot of questions for him when he woke. But he needed to rest.

I put another small log on the grate. At the foot of the bed was a thick red rug, laid out in front of the fireplace. I settled down on that, his protector. The room really was lovely and warm. It reached into me, right to my bones, healing me.

In the cave, I'd worried that I'd never feel warm again. But in the Red Room, I felt cozy, felt content, felt close to Ajay. I felt safer, oddly, with him there. The fire was growing from embers to flames that licked around the log I'd added. I didn't even need a blanket right in front of it.

I rolled over to keep an eye on Ajay. But all I could see was the carved foot of the bed, squirrels clutching nuts on the dark wood. There was something underneath, lurking amid the dust bunnies that had been allowed to breed while the staff were gone to give us privacy for my healing.

I reached for it. Something smooth and cool met my touch. It felt familiar in my hand, and I recognized the shape, the weight of the stone from the night before. It was the odd rock I'd picked up in the cave and slid into my pocket. I pulled it out.

It was part of a crude small statuette. Although the head was missing, I recognized the figure's long flowing dress immediately. It was a statue of the Lady of Levay, similar to one I'd packed up in our museum a few days ago. I stared at her headless body for a long moment.

I'd been in this room, last night, after we'd been in the cave. I'd dropped this under the bed. But I couldn't remember being here. What had happened? Why had I forgotten?

I straightened up, looking around the room. There were no footprints on this floor. That was no surprise, I was wearing slippers now, and would have been in the time I'd lost after my bath. I wandered around, looking for clues. A jacket hung on the door. I guessed it was Ajay's. Everything else looked exactly as I expected.

I sighed and wandered to the corner. The bookcase behind it looked normal, and nothing sat on the desk next to it. I pulled open the drawers, knowing it was probably pointless. One contained rulers and pens and an old roll of tape. I pulled open the other one to find a pile of papers.

I pulled out a handful of the sheets and flipped through the first few. A draft letter of reference from my mother for a gardener. A timetable of house tours. An old shopping list.

I shook my head. There were no clues here. It was ridiculous to think there might be.

I went to shove the papers back in the drawer, and dropped a few of them. Among those I picked up was an envelope, addressed to my parents and ripped neatly open. On the front was a posh-looking crest, with St. Catherine's Academy printed underneath it, along with a motto in Latin. That was my old school, before the accident.

Curious, I opened the envelope, pulled out the paper and scanned the letter.

*Dear Mr. and Mrs. Glanville,*

*In follow-up to our recent phone conversation, this letter is to give formal notice of the exclusion of your daughter, Charlotte Glanville, from St. Catherine's Academy.*

*We have not come to this decision lightly, but our policies are clear on leaving the school at night as well as on alcohol and drug use. Multiple warnings and interventions as well as two previous suspensions have proved to be ineffective in your daughter's case.*

*We regret that this step has become necessary and hope you will be able to find a more suitable educational establishment to support Charlotte's needs.*

The letter continued, going into detail on the practicalities of exclusion, explaining that no school fees for my final term would be returned to my parents, and that sort of thing, but I barely read any of that.

I'd been expelled.

Leaving the school at night; alcohol and drug use. I didn't remember any of it. I couldn't imagine getting into that kind of trouble.

I tried to remember something concrete about the school; tried to bring a room to mind, or the grounds, or some of the friends I hung out with. I found only the vague shapes of classrooms and whiteboards, which were feelings as much as they were memories. It was all so foggy. This letter was concrete proof of who I was meant to be, yet the girl it described was a stranger.

I checked the date at the top of the letter; May 2nd.

I'd been sent home in disgrace. The chill of shame made me nauseous, even though I couldn't remember being expelled or exactly what I'd done. I shoved the letter back in the envelope, opened the drawer and pushed it back into the pile of papers it had fallen out of, wishing I could un-see it.

I must have felt a hundred times worse back when it happened. I would have been so worried for my future. My life was in ruins. Perhaps that's why my mother seemed so angry with me. For two weeks after my expulsion, I'd been at home, no doubt seasick with shame. Not long after that, my father had seen me leave the house, heading for the cliffs.

I shivered, in spite of the warmth from the fire.

What if my "accident" hadn't been an accident? What if I'd tried to kill myself?

# CHAPTER TWENTY

## AJAY

"Charlotte? What on Earth are you doing on the floor?"

The voice was male, posh, and older. It drifted through my totally weird dreams of caves, Oleander, and a beautiful, ghostly woman.

"Are you all right?" the man asked.

I opened my eyes to a strange room. There was dark red wallpaper around me and a heavy red blanket over me. A tall, balding man in a cardigan crouched at the end of the bed, where a girl was stirring on the floor. She sat up and clung to his arm.

"You're okay, Daddy. You're okay. I dreamt …" It was a girl, with the upper class accent I recognized from the caves, although she no longer sounded hoarse: Charlotte. She sounded sleepy and a little panicked.

"You're okay, darling. Everything's okay."

The lights faded for a moment, before flickering back to full brightness. "I'm going to have to fix that generator," he said, and when he glanced at the light, I recognized him.

He'd run down to the shore the night before. He'd thrown a bathrobe around me and pulled me up, chucking my arm over his shoulder, and half-carrying me up toward their huge house. Levay Manor, I was willing to bet.

"In my nightmare, I thought I'd lost you," Charlotte said, gazing up at her father.

He gave her a sad smile and pushed the hair back off her face. "I'm here. You've got me. I've got you. I promise. But what are you doing in here?"

"I came in to check on Ajay, and I fell asleep."

I sat up. Pain jolted through me. I grunted and lay back again.

"Ajay?" The girl's voice. Suddenly she was at my side. A pretty white girl about my age in pink pajamas, with straight, chin-length, brown hair and a long scar down her left cheek.

"Charlotte?" I hadn't seen her properly before. Even on the beach, it had been dark, and I'd been well-confused, struggling to stay awake.

She took my hand. "I'm here. How are you?"

I moved my shoulders, shuffling on the bed. Every muscle screamed at me, including a few I'd never noticed before.

"I'm alive," I managed. "Thanks to you."

A smile lit up her face, pushing the scar deeper into her cheek, like a long, red dimple.

"You were in quite a state last night," the man said. He sounded worried. "Both of you."

"I was?" Charlotte said.

He nodded gravely.

"Um … This is my father," Charlotte gestured at him. "Peter Glanville."

"He helped me up the beach."

"Oh yes. Of course he did. Sorry."

I didn't remember much after that, other than drying off and struggling into the pajamas I was wearing now. That had taken me a ridiculously long time. I was barely there on the beach and my memories of the cave weren't much better. I tried not to feel massively embarrassed about that.

"This is Levay, isn't it?"

"That's right," Charlotte said.

"What happened to you?" her dad asked. "How did you end up here?"

I didn't want her dad to think he'd let a raving lunatic into his house, so I muttered something quickly about getting lost in the mist and falling out of my boat. He nodded, so that seemed to satisfy him.

But there was one thing I had to tell them, even if it would make me seem bananas.

"You know ... the mainland has forgotten about you?" It sounded almost normal when I said it like that. As if people forgot about islands all the time, like a cousin's birthday.

Charlotte's lips pursed a little. "What do you mean?"

"No one remembers you're here. They haven't heard of Levay."

Charlotte glanced at her father, but he was looking at me, his gaze full of sympathy.

"You've clearly been through a lot, Ajay."

Uncertainty crossed Charlotte's face. Of course it sounded daft. But what we'd been through was daft. We'd followed impossible voices in the dark. We'd found a hidden tunnel, a secret cave.

"You need to rest, Ajay," her father said.

"If ... everyone forgot, why did you remember? Why did you come here?" It hurt to hear the doubt in her voice.

"You were looking for a girl with purple hair who went missing in July, you said last night," Charlotte's father said. "What was her name? Olivia?"

I nodded, glad I'd been able to explain that much. "Oleander. The police think she ran away. I think she might have tried to come here."

"Why here?" His long fingers fiddled with the buttons on his cardigan.

"I ... found the island's name written down in her room. She was reading a book about it, and she'd made all these notes."

Charlotte's father shook his head. "I'm sorry, but she can't have come here. The ferry isn't even running."

The lamp by the bed flickered, fading out for a second then coming back. Creepy.

I nodded at the light. "What's wrong with it?"

"It's just the generator. Look, the island's been closed to the public for a while. Perhaps that's why you thought it's been forgotten? Because we aren't open?"

"There was a boat missing. On the mainland."

"You think Oleander took it?"

"I ... wasn't sure. It just seemed worth checking out."

It sounded super weak, now that someone was asking me about it. Maybe the boat had just floated away, and the bloke at the watersports place was right.

"It wasn't worth risking your life," Charlotte's father said, gently. "We haven't seen anyone else here in a while. What did she look like?"

"She had purple hair."

"Eye color?" He prompted. I concentrated, but I couldn't picture her eyes.

"I have a photo of her," I said, suddenly remembering. It had been in the waterproof pocket of my jacket, so it might still be okay. "It was in my jacket."

I sat up. It hurt, but I managed to prop myself up on the head of the bed.

"Please, don't exert yourself," Charlotte's dad said. "I'll bring your jacket. It's been hanging up."

It was on the back of the door. He passed it to me. It was damp along the seams, but the rest was dry. I reached for the water-proof pocket. It was open and empty.

I pulled it open and peered in. I poked my fingers into the corners.

I searched the other pockets and found my mask. It was soggy and ruined. I didn't feel right without it on.

"Was it a small photograph?" Charlotte's father asked.

"It was folded. It was a poster."

"A poster?"

"A missing person poster. Oleander's mother has been putting them up everywhere. Hundreds of them."

Charlotte's father's brow crinkled. "I thought you said she ran away?"

"The police think she ran away, but her mum doesn't. She won't give up looking. That's why she's put the posters up. It rained, and they got ruined. She had to put up new ones, and I helped. She's planning to get them laminated next time."

"She'll put up laminated posters of Oleander after the next time it rains?" Her father shook his head and looked at Char-lotte. "Parents will do anything for their children." He took a deep breath, and when he spoke again, his voice was heavy with sadness. "I'm sorry. This is a small island. Your friend isn't here. If there was someone other than us three, we'd know."

The stupid bit of hope I still had made me ask one more question. "Three? Who else is here?"

"There's Charlotte, my wife Eleanor, and me."

Charlotte's head twitched up at that. "Where is Mummy?"

"She went to sleep. She wasn't feeling well."

"I have to call my parents," I said.

Charlotte's father shook his head. "I wish you could, but the phones are down. They're a bit unreliable here, and we don't get mobile reception."

I felt sick at that. "They'll be worried out of their minds."

He nodded. "I would imagine so. Don't worry, as soon as the landline is working, we'll call, and we'll find a way to get you home. But for now, you both need to rest and recover. Charlotte, go back to your bedroom and try to get a little more sleep. I'll bring you all some breakfast in a couple of hours."

Charlotte's father left. Charlotte trailed behind him, looking back at me as if she didn't want to leave, and glancing at the window as she went.

Although it was nice to have her around, I was glad to be on my own. I needed to find out more about Levay Island.

This was a totally weird place. Charlotte and her father clearly hadn't noticed there was something odd going on. I wondered if their minds slid off the strangeness, like mine when I'd tried to remember Levay. Oleander could be hidden here, forgotten like the island itself. And if she was, I was determined to find her.

I would search every inch of the island for her.

# CHAPTER TWENTY-ONE

## CHARLOTTE

I wasn't sure if I should leave Ajay alone, but I felt awkward about the time I couldn't remember and he seemed okay even after the Lady's visit, so I let my father lead me back to my own bedroom.

Truthfully, I was exhausted. I wasn't sure what time I'd got back from the cave, and had no idea how long I'd been in bed, but it felt as if I'd barely slept.

My father asked a few more questions, about saving Ajay and the cave we'd found ourselves in. The whole story clearly disturbed him, and he clutched my hands so tightly it hurt, and said again and again how lucky I was to be alive.

I didn't tell him about the voices, the ghostly woman, or the statue I'd found. I'd seen how he'd reacted to Ajay's story about everyone forgetting Levay. It did sound irrational, but there was something about it that tugged at me as I climbed back into bed.

I wasn't the only one forgetting things.

I hadn't left the island in my recovery, and I wasn't sure if my parents had either, other than the occasional trip for groceries. I tried to remember the last time I'd been off Levay or anything about my "accident," but my brain was overloaded with exhaustion.

I'd be able to think clearer later, and I'd talk to Ajay about it then.

I woke abruptly. A figure stood over my bed, a woman, and for a moment I thought it was the Lady of Levay, who had drifted through my dreams. But this woman was a solid silhouette, blocking the light, which was now on.

"Who are you?" she demanded. "What are you doing in my daughter's bed?"

I scrambled to sit up, to see her properly.

"Mummy?"

The lights flicked above her, casting her face in shadow momentarily.

She was wearing the same clothes she'd been in when I'd overheard her, but her blond hair stuck up at the back and the sleeve of her white shirt was ripped. It was so unlike her that I wondered if I was still sleeping.

"Who …?" She put a hand against her head and swayed. I shoved the covers off and stood next to her, quickly. She leaned against me, eyes half-closed. She reached up to my hair like a child, and touched it gently, then ran her fingers along the collar of my pajamas.

"Charlotte? No. It's not you."

"Yes, Mummy, it's me. Let's get you back to bed."

I wanted to call for my father, but that might panic her. Instead, I put my arm around her, and helped her shuffle back to her bedroom. She leaned against me.

"Your hair smells like Charlotte," she said.

"Of course it does." I tried to keep the tremble out of my voice. I wondered if she was really drunk. Is this what my father meant when he said she was unwell? Or had the Lady of Levay been to visit her too? Had she taken something from my mother when she couldn't get what she wanted from Ajay?

I got my mother back to my parents' room and laid her down on top of the unmade bed. She rolled over slightly. I recoiled in shock.

Her hair was matted at the back, the red of blood underneath.

She twitched on the covers. I thought she was trying to roll over, at first, but her arms flailed. She jerked, her body flopping violently. Her eyes were half-closed, eyelids fluttering, only the whites visible.

"Mummy? Mummy?"

I touched her shoulder, unsure if I should hold her, or let her jerk around freely.

Tears filled my eyes. "Mummy?"

A wild lurch moved through her, and she banged her head against the headboard, hard.

"No!"

I reached for her arms to stop her hurting herself as the fit threw her around on the bed.

"Daddy!" I shouted. "Help!"

She kept writhing under my grip. She was strong, and I couldn't anticipate how she'd move. She threw me off on one side.

"Daddy! Please!"

I heard footsteps from down the hall. I let out a sob as my father came running in.

"What is it?"

"I don't know!"

My mother moved under me, but not as violently.

More footsteps as Ajay limped into the room.

"She's having a fit or something! We have to help her!" I said.

She was still shaking, but by then it was more like Ajay's trembling in the cave. One of her legs kicked, but the quaking that had seized her was calming.

I let go of her shoulders, and she lay still on the bed. There was a little blood on the pillow, from the back of her head.

"What do we do?"

Daddy stared, mouth open.

Ajay moved into the space next to me, wincing in pain. "Check her breathing. Put her in the recovery position."

I wanted to hug him for giving me something to do. I put a hand on Mummy's chest and felt it move up and down. Then I climbed onto the bed and rolled her onto her side, easing her legs and arms out to stabilize her. I looked to my father.

"I think she hit her head. You said she was ill. Was she like this?"

"I don't know. I found her outside earlier this morning. She seemed confused, and I told her to go to bed. I just thought …"

He didn't need to finish. He thought she was drunk. It wouldn't have been surprising. I'd barely seen her without a glass of something in her hand over the last few months.

But she wasn't drunk now.

I moved her hair carefully to look at the wound there. It didn't look deep; but it was hard to tell. I didn't want to touch it, for fear of making it worse.

"Maybe she'd had a fit before you found her," I said.

My father put a hand over his mouth. "I thought she just needed sleep."

"She needs a doctor," Ajay said.

We both stared at him.

"There isn't one on the island," my father said after a long pause.

"She needs to get to a hospital," Ajay said. "Can you call an ambulance from here? Or, I don't know, the coastguard?"

"The phone's still not working."

Ajay swore. "Charlotte mentioned that you have a boat, right?"

"The ferry, yes, but we can't sail in this fog, and we're low on fuel. I … I've been syphoning it off to keep the generator running. I don't think we have enough to make it to the mainland."

Silence fell on us, like a smothering blanket.

"We're trapped on the island?" I asked.

He rubbed at his forehead with his long fingers. "I … didn't want anyone to know. I didn't want you to worry. I'm sure the fog will lift soon, or the phones will start working, and we can get help."

I felt cold. "But … what about food? What were you going to do?"

"We have tinned and dry food. We'll be okay for … a week or two, maybe?"

"We have to do something!" I said.

He rubbed at his forehead. "Yes. Oh, this is bad …" After a moment, his face cleared, and he clicked his fingers. "The rain. We need the rain. We just need the rain."

"The rain?"

My father looked at me, and there was something I'd never seen in his eyes before, a manic energy. It worried me.

"The rain … might clear the mist. It often does. We just need to wait until it rains, then the mist will go and we can try to sail, or send a signal to the mainland: a flare or something."

"Are you sure?" Ajay asked.

My father nodded, vigorously. "It's a Levay thing. But it has to rain a lot."

I didn't know if he was right, or if this was just another kind of the madness that seemed to be affecting us all.

My mother had said there was something wrong with me, but there was something wrong with her, too. And it was clear it didn't stop there. Ajay had said the mainland had forgotten about us.

Something was wrong with the whole island, and we were trapped here.

I looked at my mother, still on the bed apart from the rise and fall of her chest. She needed help.

We all did.

# CHAPTER TWENTY-TWO

**AJAY**

Charlotte's dad looked well worried. He said to go back to our rooms, so I did. He was obviously having trouble holding it together. As I left, he muttered something about needing to check on the flooding in the cellar, but I guessed it was an excuse to be on his own.

I couldn't blame him for being freaked out. His daughter had almost died and his wife was seriously ill. I was glad to be alone, too. This whole thing was messed up: hallucinations in the fog, almost drowning, and Charlotte's mother, jerking in the bed like she was possessed, plus we were all trapped here.

There was something wrong about Charlotte, too.

She was on edge, and the scar on her face looked wrong. It was a red raised line down her cheek, too wide, like it hadn't been stitched properly.

It wasn't that I didn't trust her. She'd saved my life. I just didn't think she had any clue what was happening either.

Their confusion gave me a daft kind of hope. If they didn't know what was happening, they could be wrong about Oleander.

I glanced at my jacket, wishing I still had the poster. I'd been so careful to keep it in that waterproof pocket, even on the boat. Maybe I tried to take it out last night to show them when I'd been cold and confused and my hands were numb. Maybe it was just on the ground or under the bed.

I eased myself to the edge of the mattress and stood up, on embarrassingly shaky legs. I ducked down and checked under the bed. It was dark underneath, and I couldn't see all the way to the other side. So I walked around the bed. I was still totally weak, and I limped because of the fall in the cave, but I was getting better. I bent down to check under the end of the bed, but there was nothing but dust there either.

The poster must have fallen out somewhere else. Maybe on the beach. Maybe in the cave. I had been pretty delirious. I had to accept that it was lost.

I stood up too quickly and got dizzy. I grabbed onto the nearest thing — the wardrobe door handle — to steady myself. I misjudged it a bit and the door swung open, a load of boots and heels fell out, thudding onto the floor.

I bent over carefully, embarrassed, and started to put them back into the wardrobe. There was a load of other shoes piled up in there, and more fell out as I tried to fix things.

"What are you doing?" I turned. Charlotte's father stood in the doorway. He held a tray with some soup on it.

"Sorry. I was trying to see if I could walk. I got wobbly and bumped into the wardrobe."

"Best to rest, don't you think?" He put the soup on the bedside table. "But you've reminded me I need to throw those old shoes out. I should have done that a while ago."

I picked up the last of the shoes and put them back. They didn't look like old shoes. Several pairs of the heels looked pretty new. Still, if he had a thing for ladies' shoes, it was none of my business.

"Sorry," I said again, heading back to the bed and climbing in carefully. "How's your wife?"

"I … don't know. I should get back to her." He paused on the way out. "You were in quite a state last night, when you first got here." He stared at me, hard, as if he were worried I was going to get into "quite a state" now.

I cringed, wondering what I'd done or said. Maybe he thought I was mental. Maybe he thought I'd been throwing shoes around the room on purpose when he came in.

"Sorry," I said. "I don't remember anything after the beach. I … must have been, I don't know, feverish or something. I hope I wasn't … I didn't cause offense."

He relaxed a little and smiled. "Yes, I thought it was probably that. Of course you didn't cause offence. You seem a lot calmer now. Eat some food and get some rest."

I wanted to ask what I'd done that I didn't remember, but he hurried out, no doubt to look after another of his patients, so I ate the soup instead. It seemed weird to have soup for breakfast, and although it was just bland tinned lentil soup, I was so hungry it tasted almost as good as Amma's daal.

I must have been acting really crazy last night if he thought explaining that the mainland had forgotten about them and dropping shoes all over the floor was "a lot calmer."

When I was done, I laid back on the red blankets. I was exhausted. The fire was still hot, and the windows closed, with the curtains drawn. A little gray light came in through the crack. It was morning now, but Charlotte's dad was right. I needed to rest. I hurt all over.

I had no idea what was coming, but I'd need rest to face it.

I wasn't sure how much later it was when she touched my shoulder.

"Ajay," she whispered.

"Hmm?" I sat up, body still aching.

Her hair swung in front of her face as she leaned forward. "Shh. Daddy's asleep."

"How are you?" I asked.

"I'm fine. But Mummy isn't. She hasn't woken. I'm worried." She seemed twitchy, secretive.

"You want to try to take the ferry, don't you? Even after everything your dad said."

"It's worth a try. I just need someone … You know the way."

That was totally weird. "It's the mainland. Big bit of land straight ahead. Can't miss it."

"I'm not sure where the ferry goes, like, where it docks. I …" There was something about her expression. A confusion I recognized. I'd felt it when I tried to think of Levay.

"Hang on. Can you remember the mainland?"

She bit her lip. "Only vaguely. But that's not surprising. There was … um … an accident. I'm still recovering. I have amnesia."

"That's what the scar is from?"

She nodded. "That's why we closed the island. To give me time to recover."

"A head injury? Like your mum?"

She sat down on the edge of the bed, heavily. "Yes. No. I fell from the cliffs."

I kept my mouth shut. She stared at her hands in her lap. I wanted to know what she was thinking, but her expression was totally unreadable. I was starting to suspect that it wasn't just Oleander I didn't understand. I didn't understand any girls at all.

"Things are strange here. I've been forgetting things. My mother's been forgetting things. She even forgot me."

Cold crept up my back. I thought of Oleander's notes, with *forgetting* underlined and circled. I remembered what Charlotte's father had said, about me being in "a bit of a state."

She sighed. "Can I tell you something, without you thinking I'm ... messed up?"

"Yeah. 'Course."

She took a shaky breath in, like she was about to cry. "I don't know what's happening. Everything seems to be weird since my ... accident. And there's a figure in the mist, like a ghost. A woman. I think it's something to do with her. The Lady of Levay."

"A woman in, like, a long gray dress? You've seen her?"

Her head jerked up. "*You've* seen her?"

"She was in the fog when I got lost. Have you heard of Lethe?" I asked.

She looked at me like I was mad. "You mean Levay? Levay Island?"

"I mean Lethe, the Greek Goddess of Forgetting."

Charlotte shook her head.

"Oleander was looking for her. She'd read about the Lady of Levay and thought she might be ... I don't know, like a local goddess of forgetting or something."

Charlotte turned properly, putting her hands on the bed and facing me.

"The Lady's bad news. People who see her usually die. She pointed you out in the water last night, and we both almost died. And I saw her here, standing over you, when you were asleep. She was taking something from you."

"Wait. What? She was here? She was taking something? The poster?"

"No. It was like steam. Like mist, rising from you."

I shivered, totally freaked out. But I held it together.

"Memories," I said, finally.

"What?"

"I can't remember what happened last night after I got to the house. You said everyone is forgetting things. She's a goddess of forgetting. What if she's stealing our memories?"

"I can't remember what happened last night either." Charlotte stared at me for a long moment. "We have to get off the island. We have to get my parents off the island. We're all in danger."

I was totally inclined to agree with her at that point. I needed to get home to my parents too. They had to be going out of their minds with worry. But reality intruded. "Your dad said there wasn't enough fuel to make it to the mainland."

"We don't have to make it to the mainland. There are flares on the ferry. If we can get out of the fog, we can let one off."

I nodded. "Okay. Yeah. Let's get out of here. But I need to find Oleander. I know you haven't seen her, but like you said, you're forgetting things. What if she's here, and you've forgotten her?"

Charlotte looked skeptical. "She's not here. Sorry, we really would know."

"But you could have forgotten, right? The island is tiny. Can you at least take me around it quickly before we go?"

"I really need help for Mummy. And if the Lady is stealing our memories, we have to go before she can do that again. We might forget this conversation. We might have already had it!"

"If Oleander's here, she's in danger too. I can't just leave her."

She sighed. "Fine. Then we have to head out now, before the Lady comes back."

# CHAPTER TWENTY-THREE

## CHARLOTTE

I got dressed and checked on my mother. She was still sleeping, breathing so quietly I had to lean right in to hear it. That was bad.

She didn't smell like she usually did, of floral perfume and expensive moisturizer. She smelled of sweat. I wondered why my father hadn't tried to clean her hair up before I realized he was probably afraid to move her.

He was asleep on the sofa in the living room. I tiptoed past him on my way out.

Opening the door into the public areas of Levay Manor always felt like going back in time. I stepped into a hallway lined with portraits with a thick red carpet running down the center. The door I'd come through was labeled "PRIVATE" in a gothic script, making our apartment seem much more mysterious than they were.

On either side, my illustrious ancestors stared down on me, with judgmental looks fixed on their haughty faces. Perhaps they knew what dire financial straits the family was in, and how it was all my fault.

Ajay waited for me at the bottom of the stairs in his own clothes, which my father must have washed and dried. He wore his jacket over jeans and a brown jumper that suited him, just the right amount of tight on his chest. He was leaning against the wall slightly. I guessed his knee was still hurting.

"Nice jumper." I spoke in a whisper. "Are you sure you're up to this?"

He nodded, firmly.

"One quick circuit of the island, then we leave. Deal?"

Ajay nodded again. I led him through the gallery toward the side door. Ajay started slowly, wincing when he put his weight on his left leg. I wondered if I should have agreed to searching for his Oleander. This was going to take too long if he couldn't walk properly.

Halfway across the gallery, he stopped. I thought it was his leg for a moment, but he was staring past me. "It's her. It's the Lady."

I froze, but when I turned, I realized he was looking at a painting that had been taken down from the wall. We were in the process of putting it into storage. It was a full-length portrait of a woman. The face had been roughly cut out, leaving a jagged hole.

I'd never paid too much attention to it before, but now I looked, he was right. It looked just like her. Not her face, of course, since that was gone, but her figure, her long, gray dress. She'd been painted walking through trees, and her skirts, falling in folds to her feet, dragged in the leaves. I leaned in. The painter had caught something of the hazy nature of her clothes. They were almost translucent in the portrait. How had I missed that?

"What happened to it?" Ajay asked.

"It's always been ripped like that. It's famous for it."

"Who cut her face out?"

Daddy loved to lecture on this stuff. He almost seemed happy that my memory gaps meant he got to teach me all about it again, so I at least knew the answer.

"Everyone thinks the vandal was probably Captain Granger's wife. She was the daughter of the Earl at the time. The story has it that not long after their wedding, his young bride found a stack of rough sketches of an unknown woman, and this completed painting."

"I remember reading about that. But it's not just some woman he had a fling with, is it? It's the Lady. Remind me, didn't something bad happen to the captain?"

"After his wife burned the sketches and cut up the portrait, Captain Granger drowned. Everyone assumed it was suicide due to the scandal. But if that's a painting of the Lady …" I shivered. "Come on, let's keep moving."

I opened the side door carefully, to make as little noise as possible, and we slipped outside.

"Do you … think you lost any more memories? Since I last saw you."

Ajay shook his head. "No gaps, not like last night."

I exhaled. "Me neither. I don't think the Lady has been back."

We cut around the side of the house, through the long grass. I took him along the path, leading him around the way that kept us back a little from the cliffs. His limp was bad, but he could still move at a reasonable pace.

"Wow," Ajay said. "This is an amazing place."

I pointed uphill. "Let's start at the eastern clifftops. That's the highest point. You can see the whole island from up there."

Ajay looked around him as we climbed. I couldn't work out what he was looking at, until he spoke.

"How long has the island been surrounded by mist?"

I looked at the gray blanket that engulfed the island. "Daddy says it's common on Levay. Something to do the with the way the water upswells at the shore. I can't remember the last time it wasn't here."

Ajay gave me a meaningful look.

"You get used to it. It's just weather."

He looked awkward. "Look, you need to know before we try to go through it. It's not a normal mist."

"It shouldn't be here all the time?"

"Not just that, there are … things in it."

"Things?" I felt the hairs on my arms stand on end.

Ajay nodded, staring at the ground as we walked. When he spoke, it was a mumble. "Yeah. I thought I was losing it."

He looked embarrassed. It was kind of charming.

"We followed impossible voices that led us to safety in complete darkness. We survived drowning. We can handle it. What's in the mist? What's between us and the mainland?"

"Weird visions. Hallucinations, like the voices in the cave, but you can see them too. A bit like ghosts but not."

*Ghosts.* I shivered.

"The boat was old, and it broke down. I got trapped in that nightmare." He shook his head. "That's how I ended up falling out."

"Visions? Of what?"

He paused. "People and things like that. It's nasty in places, but mostly just weird and creepy. It was all mixed up like a nightmare and a dream at the same time."

"So … imaginary stuff?"

"No. I don't think so. I … think they might be things that happened. Like recordings of real things, y'know?"

"Like memories?"

He stopped dead and stared at me.

"Exactly like memories." He shook his head. "A forgotten island surrounded by a mist of memories." He shook his head. "I should have worked that one out. Duh."

I shivered. "Whose memories? Do you think … if the Lady steals memories, are they those memories?"

Ajay paused and leaned on his good leg. "I don't know. I didn't see any of my own. If they're memories, they're a lot of people's memories."

"You said people had forgotten about the island."

He nodded, slowly. "There were a load that could be from the island. But there were others too. Ones definitely not from here."

I had to say the words out loud. "To get off the island we have to sail through a fog of stolen memories, haunted by a goddess of forgetting?"

Ajay nodded. "You don't have to do it alone. I'll be there."

A tight knot of warmth formed in my gut.

We headed out onto the rise toward the cliffs, and the wind picked up. I wished my hair was long enough for a ponytail, as the breeze threw it across my eyes. I tried to push it behind my ears, even though it wasn't long enough to stay there.

The world looked like it ended a little way ahead of us, and the ghostly mist swallowed up the horizon beyond.

"Is it safe up here?" Ajay asked, glancing at the flapping yellow tape.

"I wouldn't get close to the edge if I were you. It doesn't end well. Trust me on that one." I watched the ground ahead of us for signs of weakness.

"What happened?"

"I'm not sure. Apparently, I went out for a walk last May, and didn't return. At first, they feared the worst, but they eventually found me washed up on the beach, hidden by the jagged coastline. I'd been there for a while, injured but alive. They think some of the cliff must have crumbled away."

"What did your accident do to you? Were you like your mum?"

"I don't think so. I just don't remember a lot of things."

"Like what?"

I laughed at that. "I don't know, do I? Most of my recovery is a blur. I don't remember what happened or anything much before it, and I've been waking up with gaps in my memory ever since. I thought it was due to the accident, until you came."

I pointed out the island below us; the slope down and the slight rise on the other side of the manor's valley, and where the cave's mouth would be, below us.

"That's where we got stuck yesterday?"

I nodded.

Ajay looked thoughtful, switching his gaze between the cliff edge above the cave, and the manor behind us.

"We went back in the tunnel, right?" He traced our course with his finger, under the grass below us. "Then we climbed up, and we kept going back, until we found the cave we stayed in until the tide went back out." He kept his finger moving. "About that far, right?"

He was pointing almost right at the manor.

"We were so close to home."

"Your dad said something about flooding in the basement."

"Yes. We're meant to get engineers in to stabilize the house."

He nodded. "I'm not surprised, with caves going that deep into the island. Maybe that stream runs right under the manor. Are there other caves?"

I shook my head. I pointed out the beach where we'd washed up, and the sheltered cove on the opposite side of the island, with the pier the ferry was docked at. I told him about the portrait at the house, and all I'd read on the Lady of Levay, although he already knew most of it. I told him about the people associated with her being doomed.

Ajay nodded, and his jaw moved.

"You're thinking of her, aren't you? The girl with the purple hair that you're looking for. You're wondering if she's doomed too."

"She can't be doomed. She has to be alive."

I didn't want to say the obvious. She wasn't here. She never made it here. She might have drowned, or she might have gone someplace else entirely. But I didn't need to say anything. Ajay could see how small the island was, how impossible it would be for another person to be here, and for us not to know.

He was silent for a long time before he wiped at his face. "I guess we should head to the ferry."

I nodded, and we started to walk back downhill. "Tell me about Oleander."

And he did. It was obvious he'd been wanting to talk about her from the start. He told me about meeting her in the gift shop she'd worked at as we stumbled our way back downhill. He told me about their Saturday lunchtimes together, joking and laughing, how she always got his sense of humor, the way they understood each other, and I found myself almost jealous at the light in his eyes when he spoke about her.

As we crept past the manor again, he told me about what happened to her father, and the way she blamed herself for his suicide.

"That's ridiculous," I said. "Her father should never have put that all on her. She wasn't his therapist."

Ajay shrugged. "I tried to tell her that. She wouldn't believe me, or her mum. It ate away at her, you know? And I understand that. She felt responsible for her dad, and that made her such an easy target for someone like Rupert."

"Rupert?"

Ajay looked even sadder. He shook his head. "That's another story. I … don't want to go into that now."

"What did Oleander look … sorry, what does she look like, exactly?"

"I can give you the exact description from the poster I lost if you want. I put up so many I memorized it."

I nodded.

He took a deep breath and recited the words in a flat voice. "Oleander Dillon, seventeen years old, 5'5". Last seen July twentieth at around three p.m. on Southcliff Pier. Purple ombré hair. Wearing a gray shirt, jean shorts, and purple Converse trainers."

I stopped dead, cold spreading through me.

"What is it?"

The wind picked up, hissing through the small scrubby trees. "Purple Converse?" I asked.

"Yes. High tops."

I swallowed. The grass whispered around us. I saw him from the corner of my eye watching me, expectantly, caught between hope and fear.

"I ... saw a trainer like that. A purple one."

"Where?"

I turned to him. I wanted to hold his hand or something, to break the news more gently, but even after the hours I'd spent keeping him warm, I didn't know him well enough.

"In the mouth of the cave. When we were getting out. I tripped over it."

He stood still for one long second, then started sprinting downhill.

"No, Ajay! Wait!"

# CHAPTER TWENTY-FOUR

## AJAY

She shouted after me, but I couldn't hear what she was yelling. Blood pumped in my ears. I sprinted downhill, stumbling on the lumpy ground. I wouldn't have stopped if I was in better shape.

My bad knee gave way. I hit the ground hard with my bruised and scraped hands, then rolled over the stony grass, pain at my shoulder and chest. I came to a stop, and curled up for a moment, determined not to make an idiot of myself and cry. It was hard not to.

Charlotte reached my side. "Are you okay?"

I couldn't say anything, physical and emotional pain colliding.

Charlotte sat next to me. I felt her hand on my shoulder.

"Stupid question." She sighed. "Look, it's just a shoe, okay? Probably nothing. Could have been anyone's. But we'll tell the authorities. As soon as we get help."

I nodded, not trusting myself to speak.

"Okay. Rest for a minute, then we'll go."

I wanted to go to the cave. I wanted to see for myself. But that was daft. Oleander hadn't been in there last night. If she'd been washed into that cave, it was way too late for her, and Charlotte's mother needed help. There was still time to save her.

It probably wasn't Oleander's shoe anyway. Almost for sure, right?

It was a couple of minutes before I could pull myself together. Charlotte didn't hurry me, although she kept glancing across the island toward the ferry cove. I tried to wipe my eyes on my sleeve without her seeing. When I looked up, she was staring off at the misty horizon.

"Let's go," I said.

She offered me a hand. I waved it away, which was stupid. But she saw me struggling and took my arm anyway. She put an arm around my back and helped me half-hop, half-limp.

The island dipped in the middle. It rose steeply on the left up to the manor, then to the high cliffs we'd been at. On the right, the land formed a softer hillside. We walked through the valley. Charlotte steered us between trees and bushes, keeping us out of sight of the manor as we headed for the cove.

It felt far. I was weaker than I wanted to admit.

"I hope Daddy doesn't worry," Charlotte said, and glanced back at her home.

I thought of Pa and Amma and guilt slammed into me. They'd lost one child thanks to my idiocy. What had they been going through since yesterday?

I hobbled along faster. Charlotte was right. We had to get out of here.

It took ages to reach the cove. It was more sheltered than the beach I'd washed up on, but just as overcast and foggy, even though it was probably only early afternoon. This place, the way it was always so cloudy, messed with my head and my sense of time.

The ferry sat low in the water. It was about the size of a bus, with "LEVAY FERRY" printed on the side in big letters, stained with lines of rust. It had benches for seating around the edge of the inside, some of it under the cover of a fiberglass roof that stretched halfway across the boat. At the front, there was a proper cabin for the captain. Charlotte led me down the short pier toward it.

The pier was made of old wood, and I trod gingerly in some places, where it felt soft under my shoes. A few planks were fresh, standing out like fake teeth in a rotted mouth, and there was a stack of lumber nearby. I guessed they'd been fixing the pier while the island was closed.

There was a gate on the side of the boat, and a ramp that lowered down to bridge the gap between the pier and the ferry, but it was fixed in the "up" position it would have been in at sea.

We both struggled with it before I found a pin on the side of the ramp, next to the handrail, and pulled it out. The ramp was heavy, but we lowered it onto the pier together, and hurried to the ferry.

Charlotte reached the pilot's cabin before me. She tugged at the door, then stopped to look properly at it.

"It's locked," she said.

"Do you know where the keys are?"

She shook her head, and the pointlessness of our quest sank in.

"We'll need keys to get in the cabin and probably to operate it too. Have you ever driven the ferry?"

"No." She rubbed at her forehead. "We … can't get off the island, can we?"

I was about to shake my head when something caught my eye. Something bobbing in the water, just a little further along the shore, behind the rocks that jutted out at the end of the cove.

"Look," I said, pointing.

There was no way we'd have seen it from the shore, or even the pier, hidden as it was by the jagged coastline. I limped over to the very front of the ferry to see properly.

It was the stern of a small boat, floating on the tide.

It took us a while to get down to the boat. We had to skirt around the shoreline and then back inland, clamber between some stones, and down to an area that was too small to call a cove or a beach. It was just a little gap in the rocks. We would never have found the boat if we hadn't seen it from the ferry.

It took me longer than it should have to get there, and I was exhausted by the time we made it. My bad knee ached. Charlotte was trying not to look impatient, but I was slowing her down.

It was a little dinghy with a small motor, luckily in better shape than the one I'd taken to the island, tied to a rock.

"What's this doing here?" Charlotte asked.

"It doesn't belong to your family?"

"No. My father would have mentioned it."

"If he remembered it," I said.

She nodded as that sank in. "Is it safe?"

"It's floating," I said, "but there's only one life jacket."

"There'll be more on the ferry," she said. And before I could offer to get one, she'd hurried off. She was back so quickly I felt embarrassed over how long I'd taken to get down to the hidden bay. She gave me the one she'd got, and I put it on.

I used the rope to pull the boat closer to us. Charlotte clambered into it and it rocked wildly. I got in awkwardly after her as she fastened her life jacket, almost tipping the whole thing. I slumped onto a bench seat. A can of baked beans rolled out from underneath. I picked it up.

"Is this the boat your parents used to restock at the mainland, before the mist?"

Charlotte shrugged. "Sorry. I don't remember."

Charlotte's father had mentioned they had tinned and dried food, and I remembered the soup for breakfast. Maybe they were out of bread or milk for cereal. How long had it been since any of them had left the island?

Charlotte settled at the back end of the boat, by the engine. Part of me wanted to offer to drive, or whatever the boat term for it was, but it would be pathetic bravado.

I wasn't okay.

The night in the cave had done serious damage, and the news about Oleander's shoe had unnerved me. I clutched the side of the boat as I struggled to undo the rope from the rock. Fortunately, it was less complicated than the one back at the water-sport center. As soon as it was clear, Charlotte started the boat's propeller. After a few tugs, the engine sputtered into life.

She steered us into the nearest rocks with a bang, then got us pointing out to sea. The growl of the engine drowned out the whispers of the mist and she turned before we reached it, driving between the fog and the cliffs as they rose to the right of us. They were so high I wondered how she survived falling from them.

If that was really what happened to Charlotte. With a goddess of forgetting around, you didn't need a brain injury to get amnesia on Levay.

I wondered why Charlotte didn't head into the fog. It took me a while to realize she was heading around to the opposite side of the island, the one I'd washed up on. It made sense. That was the side of the island the mainland was on. But it was also the side where the cave was. The cave where Charlotte had seen a purple trainer.

The tide was out. Almost as far as when we'd left the cave. I saw the black gap in the cliffs appear to the side of us. We had to go right past it anyway.

"Charlotte!" I had to shout over the engine. She looked at me. "Can we check the cave?"

She pointed at her ears. "What?"

I shouted louder, leaning toward her, "Can we have a look in the cave? Quickly? I just want to see if it was Oleander's trainer, if it's still there."

Charlotte glanced at the mist then back at me. She was in a hurry. I was too, but I had to know.

"Please?"

"Okay. But we'll have to be quick." Charlotte steered around until the dark gap of the cave opened wider ahead of us, a strip of sand in front of it. She cut out the engine again as we approached, and let our momentum carry us in.

The boat ran aground gently. We splashed into the cold of the ankle-deep sea and pulled the boat above the waterline. The cave waited in front of us, a mouth.

"Where was the trainer?"

Charlotte pointed to the left, near the entrance. She shivered as we stepped out of the weak sun into the shade of the cave.

The flash of purple caught my eye. I ran over. It was still there, half buried. Purple Converse, just like Oleander had been wearing. I fell to my knees on the wet ground and picked it up. It was soaking, filled with wet sand.

It looked just like Oleander's, laces frayed and about the right size, too.

Words stumbled out of my mouth.

"Might not be hers. Even if it is, doesn't mean anything. Maybe she went for a swim, and left them on Southcliff Beach, and the tide brought them here. She could've just bought another pair and, like, gone to live in another city or something."

"I'm so sorry," Charlotte said.

"We don't know. Not for sure. We don't. What's that?"

Next to the shoe was something that looked like the tip of a white shell, but not quite. It stuck out a bit, glistening in the wet sand of the cave floor. Maybe it was something else of Oleander's. Maybe it would tell me where she had really gone.

I tried to pick it up.

It was too slippery for me to get a proper grip on it, and heavier than I'd expected. It wasn't a shell; it was bigger and mostly buried. I pulled harder. Part of it came up. It was gritty, but pale patches showed through the sand. For a moment, I thought it was just a weird branch: a long main bit, with five twigs sprouting at the end.

The horror didn't kick in then. Even with the familiar shape in front of me, it took my brain a moment to understand what I was holding.

It was a skeletal arm, buried in the wet sand.

# CHAPTER TWENTY-FIVE

## CHARLOTTE

Ajay stumbled away, dropping the thing he'd been holding. He fell backward, revealing what he'd unearthed: a mostly-rotted human arm.

My hands went to my mouth. A body. There was a body under the sand.

Oleander's body.

For a long moment, I couldn't move, paralyzed with horror. Ajay sat there, shaking his head. Finally, I was able to step toward him. I wanted to say something. I had no idea what to say. Words didn't cut it. Words didn't even begin to touch what they should.

Oleander had been dead for months.

I slumped onto the sand at Ajay's side. I put one hand on his back and felt him shaking with silent sobs.

We sat that way for a long time. The damp sand soaked my trousers. I stared at Ajay's shoulders, at his legs splayed out in front of him. I rubbed at his back, uselessly.

I couldn't bear to look at the arm of the corpse in the sand.

Every so often, Ajay wiped at his face with his sleeve. His nose was running, and he wiped that as well as the tears.

We'd probably have stayed there longer, if I hadn't heard a clonking noise from the cave mouth. I peered over my shoulder, and saw the boat, lifted by the waves that were coming in, bumping against the foot of the cliffs.

I jumped up and rushed to the boat, catching it, and holding it still before the sea could snatch it away.

"Ajay," I tried to keep my voice soft.

He looked up and saw the encroaching tide. He turned back to the exposed arm that lay on the wet sand. "We can't just leave her here."

I thought about going to tell my father. But what could he do? And if we didn't get off the island the Lady might get to us, and we'd forget. This might not even be the first time we'd found Oleander.

Our only chance was on the mainland, away from Levay.

"We'll get help for her too. They'll need to bring investigators to find out what happened."

"I shouldn't have pulled up ..." He gestured at the arm.

"Let's re-bury it ... her for now. Then the tide won't destroy the site."

I didn't want to say *grave*.

I pulled the boat up onto dry land, just inside the cave. Together, we gently covered the arm with sand. I felt we should have patted it firmly down or something, to stop the tide washing away the loose handfuls and to preserve the body for forensics or whatever, but I wasn't sure how Ajay would take it.

This wasn't really about protecting the evidence for him. It was a mini-funeral.

When we were done, he stood there as the tide rolled further into the cave, a steady drumbeat that added to the claustrophobia

I felt. It lapped slowly over the sand that hid her body, and once again lifted the dinghy.

I didn't want to join Oleander, but I couldn't rush Ajay. I held the boat against the tide that tried to tug it away again. I waited until the waves were soaking through my shoes and panic was building in my skull.

"I'm sorry," I said. My voice cracked with tension. I tried to moderate it. "We have to go now. We can tell people where to find her."

He nodded, but still didn't move. My fear screamed at me as the sound of the waves began to fill the cave, just like the night before. I fought my urge to grab Ajay and drag him to the boat.

Finally, he turned and wandered over like we had all the time in the world. He held it for me and gestured into it.

"It's okay," I said, too brightly. "You get in first."

I wasn't sure I trusted him not to just stay in the cave once I was on board, to drown with his Oleander. But he didn't argue, and climbed in. I pushed it out into the deeper water at the mouth of the cave, and he took my hand and helped me climb in, the boat rocking with the waves and my weight.

I got the engine started before the tide could push us back into the cave, and I lowered the propeller into the water, just enough to get us going. As soon as I was sure the sea was deep enough, I put the propeller all the way down, and gunned it, determined to get away from the deadly cave before it could drag us back in.

I looked back at the island as we pulled away. The mist stole the green of the valley behind us, turning it to gray.

The fog hung thick ahead. The sun was blotted out, an anemic disk. Little light got through, giving a grainy, black and white impression reinforced by a churning, gray sea.

The color left Ajay's face too, like the last of a sunset, and fear shone in his eyes, along with the grief. He wrapped his arms around himself and stared at the dark bank of clouds ahead.

I wanted to move closer to him, to hold him or hug him or something. But someone had to drive the boat. I fought my instincts and kept my hand steady on the engine, steering us toward the gloom. It helped, thinking I was doing it for him and my mother. Bravery can be funny like that. It's easier to be brave when someone else needs you to be.

The air grew thicker, damper. I became aware of another sound around us, quiet under the roar of the engine, but insistent. A sound that echoed the hiss of the water, the waves on the shore behind us. A whispering sound, like voices at a distance.

I shivered. Ajay reached for the edge of the boat and clutched it, knuckles white as he stared out into the blankness beyond. There was nothing but grayness ahead. Even though Ajay was sunk in his own world of grief, I was glad he was there. I wouldn't have wanted to face the fog alone.

The voices grew distinct, even over the engine. I heard someone sobbing, someone shouting, and a child laughing.

Dread rose in me. Not just at the unknown, at the uncanny weirdness of it all, but a different kind of dread. A feeling, deep at my core that there was something in the mist that I wasn't meant to see.

Ajay's body was tense, and as we hit each wave he jolted in his seat. I wanted to ask if he was okay, but it was such a stupid question.

"We'll get through this." The shake in my voice betrayed my words.

The mist swirled as it began to consume us whole. I glanced back, but the beach had disappeared. We were alone in the strange fog. I kept my hand hard on the tiller. I had to steer straight, but there were no fixed points to aim toward. The mist diffused the light of the sun so much I couldn't even be sure where it was.

The voices were getting louder, enough to make out what they were saying over the growl of the engine: random snatches of conversation; directions, questions, arguments. Waves slapped against the front of the boat. Small ones, but big enough to flick their chill into my face.

An image formed. Hazy at first, it coalesced into the figure of a man. He wore an old-fashioned uniform and reached out toward someone beyond the boat. I turned around but there was nothing there. When I looked back, the man fell to his knees, clutching his chest as if he'd been hurt, but there was no blood, no sign of injury. He faded away again, back into the mist.

Ajay glanced at me for the first time since the shore.

"I saw it," I said, my voice shaking a little. "It's not your imagination."

He nodded, turning back to the fog. He stared into the dark, intently.

"Are you looking for something?"

He wiped at his face. "I … the last time I was here, I saw her. Oleander. Just quickly. She was crawling in the mist."

My heart ached for him.

Tendrils of fog twisted closer to the boat, as if growing bolder. Other figures formed, shapes at first, then details grew clearer, faded colors and features coming into focus, along with smells: hay and grass, roasted meat and perfume.

To the left of the boat, a man walked with a baby in a carrier on his front, one tiny hand sticking out and clutching his finger as he murmured to the bundle.

I reflexively steered away from the pair, afraid the boat might hurt them somehow. I tried to correct course, to focus on our direction, but it was hard to find a fixed point in the mist that swirled and changed as much as the sea beneath us.

None of the memories seemed to notice us, although they acted out their odd pantomimes all around the boat like an immersive nightmare, so many different ghostly scenes, some banal, some beautiful, like a wedding taking place in Levay Manor's Great Hall. Some strange, like a bloodless battle that raged around us. Most of the figures wore modern clothes, although a few wore what looked like costumes: long dresses and ruffs around necks.

Through it all, Ajay stared ahead, looking for the ghost of the girl he obviously loved, the girl who lay buried in the cave behind us. I tried to focus on the engine, on keeping the tiller straight, glad I had something to do. I hadn't expected the mist to be this deep.

Then I noticed the waves. The prow was no longer cutting into them, and we weren't riding the rises up and down like small hills. They hit the side of the boat, tipping us, making us unsteady. I'd got turned around somehow. I was sailing parallel to the tide. How long had I been doing that? I pushed on the tiller and corrected our course.

Ajay was shaking. I wasn't sure if it was grief, or cold.

"I'm here, okay?"

He nodded, not breaking his vigil.

The haunted show played out, characters lurching out of the mist. A woman went down on one knee. She held out a ring to a delighted lady in a blue dress.

Ajay kept staring into the fog, shaking harder. He wasn't fully recovered. He should be in bed. But he wasn't safe on Levay.

A wave hit the left side of the boat hard, splashing my face, bringing my attention back to the sea. I'd overcompensated. I was sideways to the waves again, but the other way around. The figures in the mist were confusing me, messing with my sense of direction.

I righted the boat. My hands ached from clutching the vibrating tiller so hard. How long had we been trapped in the fog? Would we ever get out?

Then I saw her.

The Lady — the goddess, if Ajay was right. She was clearer, more real than the memories. I steered toward her, instinctively. She was escape, I knew it, she would free us from these horrors. She would take it all away, erase it, make things okay.

The mist grew deeper, pressing in on all sides, until even the hallucinations were swallowed by the fog, leaving us alone in the gray dark, with the woman flitting across the water ahead of us. The voices, the whispers dimmed, gave us relief for a moment.

Then there was a purr from the fog in front of us.

My hand slipped on the tiller, and we turned sharply.

Ajay turned to me. "What is it?" He shouted over the roar of the motor, but the engine cut out, so the last words fell into the suddenly silent mist, too loud.

The sound came again. I twitched around, trying to work out where it was coming from. The smell came then, of exhaust and petrol. My breath caught.

"I don't know."

"Why did you stop?"

"I didn't. The engine cut out. But we have to go a different way," I said.

"Why?"

The purring was right in front of us. But it felt more like a growl.

"There's something bad here."

"I don't think any of this can hurt us."

The mist formed into a squat shape ahead of us. The exhaust smell grew stronger, until I started to worry that the fog was toxic.

"We … can't go here."

"Where?"

"I … don't know." I started the engine again. It spluttered back into life, and I turned us away from the shape that was clearly a low building. I tried to ignore the nausea flooding my system.

Ajay had to shout to be heard over the engine as I accelerated away. "But … isn't that the way we have to go?"

"We can go around."

"Did you see the Lady?" Ajay asked. "I think she was leading us."

Why had I been following her? "She's leading us to our deaths."

"I … don't think so."

"Or something worse."

The fog felt thicker, less like water vapor, more like something solid, that held me in the spot. The shape was ahead of us, the low building. It had found us again, somehow. There was something terrible in there, I could feel it. Something too awful to see.

The engine cut out again. I swore.

"What are you doing?"

"It's not me!"

I was consumed with a need to get away. But we floated on, helpless as we drifted toward the squat building. There was a small door in the side of it, a large door at the front: a garage.

"This is wrong! Can't you feel it?"

Ajay shook his head, focused on me.

"We have to get out of here." I reached for the engine, pulled the cord to start it back up. It gave a spluttering, wet sound. I pulled again. The same. My heart started to pound.

It was too wet. The fog had got in it. I'd driven us into a trap.

I pulled at the cord again and again, frantic. Ajay was suddenly next to me, the boat rocking with his movement. He grabbed my hand. "I don't think it'll work. I thought my boat broke down because it was old. But maybe it was the mist."

I barely heard him. The waves slapped the back of the boat, pushing us on. We were at the side door of the garage. It opened before us, and we floated through. There was another shape in the mist: a car.

Fear choked me. "We have to get out of here. Please. Please!"

Ajay glanced ahead of us, to the car. He inhaled sharply. "Do you know what this is?"

"No. But it's bad. We … we can't." My words came out in a sob.

"It's okay. It's okay. It can't hurt you. It's not real."

Panic was taking over, as the waves carried us toward the car. I turned, scrambling frantically to get further back in the boat, away from it.

"Charlotte!"

Blood pounded in my ears. I glanced back over my shoulder. The garage door was opening. The car grew clearer. I closed my eyes. I couldn't see. I mustn't see.

I turned to the dark water lapping at the back of the boat. I took a deep breath.

"Charlotte! No!"

Ajay's arms wrapped around my waist, stopping me throwing myself into the sea. He held me. I screamed and flailed. I clawed at the back of the boat, trying to get a grip on it, trying to drag myself over. Ajay pulled hard, and we both fell back into the body of the boat, rolling over each other in the belly of the dinghy as it rocked wildly.

Ajay landed on top of me. I cried out and I tried to shove him off. He wasn't strong; probably still weak from hypothermia, but he used his weight to hold me down, arms wrapped around my shoulders.

"It's okay. Close your eyes. I'll look after you."

There was a scream. It was my voice, but it didn't feel like I was the one making the noise. I shut my eyes tight. I clamped my hands over my ears.

Ajay stroked my hair. He whispered to me. I couldn't hear what he was saying, but I could feel his warm breath on my cheek, his body solid and reassuring on mine. I focused on him, holding me there, keeping me safe. I tried to push out every other thought. Tried to think only of Ajay.

I stayed like that for a long time, glad for his comfort, but unable to move.

Slowly, the smell of exhaust faded, and the panic with it. I came back to myself. I let my arms relax, and uncovered my ears, keeping my eyes shut.

Ajay was still holding me down, but it felt good to be in his arms; it felt safe.

"It's gone. It's over," Ajay was saying.

I was shaking. I could feel him shaking. I opened my eyes. He was still lying on top of me, his kind face inches away, worry in his gaze.

"What was that?"

"You were right," he said. "It was something bad."

"What?"

His eyes flitted over my face as if looking for an answer. "That was Oleander's memory."

"But why did it feel like that? Why didn't it affect you?"

"I … don't know." He looked embarrassed, and moved off me, gently. Cold entered the space he left. I wrapped my arms around myself, fighting the urge to ask him to come back, to hold me again.

Ajay coughed, a little awkward. He shuffled to the back of the boat. "Let's see if the engine's working," he said. "We need to get out of here. Do you want me to steer?"

I nodded. "Thank you for being here. Thank you for saving me."

"No probs."

He settled onto the bench at the back of the boat, while I sat on the one in the middle.

"Which way were we going?"

I looked around. The mist still hid the sun and the shore. The waves went up and down, and I couldn't tell which direction they were headed anymore. The tide could have turned, anyway.

"I don't know. Just pick a direction. We can't stay here."

He gave the engine cord a hard yank, and this time it sputtered into life. He gunned the engine, and drove straight, prow cutting into the waves.

The suffocating closeness of the mist lessened. I wondered if we were finally heading the right way.

"I'm really sorry," I said.

"It's fine. You —" His mouth was open, mid-sentence. I twisted around, following his gaze to the front of the boat. If I'd been talking, I'd probably have stopped too.

There was a figure in front of us, formed out of the insubstantial mist. Her back was to us, but I knew that hair, those clothes.

It was me.

# CHAPTER TWENTY-SIX

## AJAY

The ghost version of Charlotte had her back to us, but it was totally her.

The real Charlotte sat in front of me. I watched her, afraid she might try to hurl herself into the sea again, but she seemed calm, staring at her misty doppelgänger.

"Are you okay?"

Charlotte nodded, not taking her eyes off the apparition. "I think we need to see this."

I cut the engine and let the boat carry us toward mist-Charlotte.

"You can see me too, right?" Charlotte said.

"Yeah."

Mist-Charlotte was speaking. Well, swearing. She had an impressive blue streak, but she didn't sound right. The accent was posh, if anything, a bit posher than Charlotte's real accent, but her voice was different.

I'd seen this memory before, last time I'd been in the mist, but I hadn't known Charlotte back then. Didn't something bad happen?

Mist-Charlotte turned around, and the world froze when I saw her face.

It wasn't Charlotte.

The real Charlotte gasped, staring at her imposter. Her hair and clothes were right, but she wore the face of a stranger. It was totally creepy, like a deepfake.

A hand swung from the side and connected with mist-Charlotte's face. Real-Charlotte gasped. Mist-Charlotte stumbled back and another blow came, and another, until she fell.

The momentum of the boat carried us on, past the vision.

Real Charlotte leaned over the edge of the boat and watched the apparition until it was out of sight.

"What just happened?"

"No idea." I was ready to grab Charlotte if she tried to do something idiotic again, but she just clutched the side of the boat, staring out into the mist.

The fog was silent, like it had shown us everything it wanted to. It grew thinner, and another hiss came, the natural hiss of waves breaking on the beach. I got excited for a second, but that only made it more of a letdown when I saw the shoreline.

It was the one we'd left. The pier was right in front of us. We'd sailed around the island and got precisely nowhere.

"We're back," I said, wondering if Charlotte wanted to try again.

She nodded, grimly. "The mist won't let us leave. Maybe we can try again, another time. Maybe Daddy's right, and the rain will clear it. Maybe Mummy will be okay until —"

She started sobbing.

I knew how she felt. I wanted to give her a hug or something, but we were too close to the dock. I focused on steering the boat against the opposite side of the pier from the ferry. Once we were there, I climbed off to tie it up the best I could and helped Charlotte out. She was shaking.

I was shaking too. I put my arm around her shoulder. She kept hold of me as we walked along the dock. My knee still hurt. I went slowly, limping.

The manor came into sight at the center of the island, darkened by evening drawing in. It felt like a different building to the one we'd left.

I'd been so stupid. I'd thought I might find Oleander, safe somehow. Charlotte thought she could get help for her mother. We'd both thought we could leave Levay. We should have known it wouldn't be that easy. We'd returned broken, hopeless, and trapped.

"What did any of that mean?" Charlotte asked.

"Wish I knew."

She leaned into me, wet and cold. "That was me. Except it wasn't."

"Yeah."

"I thought those were memories. But if they were, who was she?"

"I dunno."

"What's happening?"

"We'll work it out. I promise." I felt like crap saying that, because I'd already promised to get her off the island, and that wasn't happening.

"There are books, back at the house. Exhibits too. More information on the Lady of Levay or Lethe or whatever. There must be something that will make sense of all this. And we should tell Daddy."

"All of it?"

Charlotte paused. "We should warn him about the Lady and tell him about what happened to … Oleander."

Charlotte's voice was soft when she said her name. I swallowed, focusing on the ground, on walking, on anything to help me keep it together.

Charlotte continued. "But … maybe we shouldn't tell Daddy about the girl in the fog. The one who looked like me."

I nodded. I wanted to get back to the house. I didn't want to fall apart on Charlotte again, not now that she was struggling. I had to get her to her dad, and I had to be alone.

Charlotte walked slowly, shivering. The wind cut through my damp clothes, and I kept my arm around her, for warmth as well as mutual support.

We didn't bother creeping back into the manor. I doubted we'd have managed to be quiet. I was clumsy with cold and my limp, and Charlotte was dazed. We left damp and sandy footprints on the marble floor of the grand entrance hall.

Charlotte led me to some back stairs, and we went up together to her family's wing.

"Daddy," Charlotte called out as she opened the door.

No answer came. The corridor was dark, with closed doors on either side. It was completely silent.

"Daddy?" A hint of worry crept into her voice.

Charlotte approached the door at the end of the corridor, the room her mother was in. She knocked.

"Daddy?"

She put her hand on the doorknob. She pushed it open slowly, reluctantly. The room on the other side was dark. Charlotte flicked the light on. Dust hung in the still air.

Charlotte's mother was still on the bed, under the blankets.

"Where's Daddy?" Charlotte asked, voice trembling. "He should be looking after her." She hesitated on the threshold before stepping into the room.

I hovered in the doorway, feeling useless. I wanted to support her but I wasn't going in her parents' room without their permission, especially with her ill mum in there.

Charlotte approached the bed. She looked down at her mother. After a long while she turned to me, eyes wide and frightened.

"Ajay, I need you."

I hurried over. She grabbed my arm, so tight it hurt.

"I ... I don't think she's breathing." She nodded at the bed. "Please. I ... can't."

The blanket was still, the woman under it pale.

Charlotte let go of me and put a hand over her mouth. "Please," she said, voice muffled. "Please let her be okay."

I couldn't even remember what side of the neck you were meant to look for a pulse, but as soon as I touched her, I knew it didn't matter.

The body was already cool.

# CHAPTER TWENTY-SEVEN

## CHARLOTTE

I woke late afternoon, sun streaming through the window. I had a few seconds of wonderful ignorance before my brain came into focus. My cheek hurt, and my muscles ached. Then it all came crashing down on me, confused and painful, a tangle as deep and dense as the fog we'd just escaped.

My mother, dead in her bed. The girl in the mist who wasn't me. But somehow, the worst thing was the car in the garage. The dread of it still chilled me, along with regret and bone-deep shame.

I prodded at my memories of the night before for what came next, after we'd got home, but there was a hole there, again. I remembered finding Mummy's body, and Ajay checking for a pulse. I remembered him breaking it to me, gently. Then … nothing.

I examined my aches and pains, remembering where I'd got each of them, apart from the tender patch on my cheek. It could have come from the boat, from when Ajay struggled to stop me flinging myself into the water, but I wasn't sure.

I was dressed in the clothes from the day before and lying on top of the sheets. That explained why I didn't remember getting ready for bed. But I should remember returning to my room, at least.

I cursed myself, silently. We should have stayed together. We could have slept in shifts, Ajay, my father, and I to keep an eye out for the Lady, to watch over each other and stop her taking our memories.

Then it hit me. I hadn't seen my father since we'd got back, and I had no idea where he was.

I swung out of the bed and onto my sore legs. I sprinted into the hall. My parents' door was closed, and I couldn't bear to open it again.

I called out instead. "Daddy?"

"Charlotte!"

The voice came from the living room, and I hurried there, fighting back tears of relief.

"Daddy!"

He got up from a high-backed armchair by the fire. His eyes were red, and there were dark circles under them. He ran toward me and hugged me tightly.

"I was worried," I muttered into his chest. "We came back and you weren't here."

He pulled away. Held me at arm's length and looked into my eyes. "You don't remember?"

I focused on his mouth. It was surrounded by the gray of stubble, making my usually smart father look dirty. I shook my head slowly.

"Here, sit." He cleared a plate away and waved at the armchair opposite. I slumped down into it, and he took his seat again. "What do you remember?"

"We tried to leave ... We couldn't."

My father nodded. "You told me about that. Visions in the mist, you said." He looked skeptical, and I couldn't blame him. "It was a terrible idea. You could have drowned."

"I was trying to get help."

His mouth twitched. For a second, he looked uncharacteristically angry, and I found myself flinching back.

"I'm sorry," I said quickly. "I left you alone to deal with Mummy. I know you were waiting for the rain, but ..."

His shoulders slumped. "I'm sorry too. It didn't come soon enough. I ... thought she had more time. I didn't realize how bad ... I should've ... I don't know." He put his head in his hands.

I leaned forward, wondering what I could say. I wasn't as upset as him. Shouldn't I be heartbroken? Instead, I felt ... yes, sad that she'd died. Sad that I couldn't save her, but not grief-stricken. I'd seen my mother's body, but I'd not lost it, like Ajay had over Oleander, or like my father.

What was wrong with me?

I could be numb, or in denial. Perhaps I was overwhelmed, perhaps it was too much to process at once. Or perhaps it was because my mother and I didn't get on. She'd barely been able to look at me since the accident. She'd said I'd come back wrong.

Cold crept up my back. That wasn't all she'd said.

When I'd last spoken to her, she'd said I wasn't Charlotte.

My skin prickled. I'd blamed it on her head injury, on the memory loss we all had, but what if she was right? I'd thought of the other Charlotte as a fake "me." I'd thought her face didn't fit her clothes, her hair. But what if that was the wrong way around?

What if I was the "wrong" Charlotte?

I felt like I was underwater, pressure building in my ears.

My father started to sob. I patted his knee, uselessly.

"What am I going to do?" he said.

I had no idea.


I helped my father to the library. He said he needed some time to think. He seemed broken, and when I left him, he was sitting on a chair, staring into space. I asked if I could help, but he shook his head. He thanked me and apologized several times. I had no idea what he thought he was apologizing for, but I reassured him, mechanically, feeling cut off from him. As if he were just out of reach.

I checked on Ajay. I desperately wanted to talk to him. He hadn't woken yet, so I let him sleep. He needed to rest, to heal. I sat with him for a couple of hours in case the Lady came back. But he slept soundly and the room remained empty. It felt pointless. I'd already lost my memories. I was willing to bet that she'd taken everything she wanted from us for now.

I stared at the windows, hoping for rain, but the fog was still there, hovering offshore, containing the other Charlotte.

I had no idea what to do.

I felt like the ground was shifting under my feet, that it wouldn't support me. I felt like the world was crumbling and I needed something to hold on to. I kept thinking of that other Charlotte in the mist. The more I thought about it, the more I knew she was the one who fit here, not me.

I needed some answers, and it was time to find them.

There weren't many family photos in our apartment in the private part of the manor. Just three in the living room. One with my parents holding a standard-issue baby who could have grown up to be any white person. The next picture was of the three of us sitting on the beach, in silhouette. The back of my head looked right, but that didn't tell me much. Not-Charlotte had looked just like me from behind.

There was a photo of me blowing out pink candles on the cake at my seventh birthday, but it was grainy, taken in the dark with only the candle lighting my face. My cheeks were full of air, distorting my features.

I searched the shelves but that was it. There were no other family photos. I wandered down the corridor, noticing the empty nails on the wall, on rectangles of unfaded wallpaper with holes where the nails should be: the ghosts of frames. There clearly should be pictures there. Who had taken them down? Was it the Lady?

Could she touch things? Photos were memories of a kind after all.

I paused at the door of the room where my mother lay, but I couldn't bring myself to go in. I couldn't search a room with a body lying there. I couldn't remember seeing any photos there anyway.

I wandered back to the main house. The pictures there were all old portraits. I walked up and down the hallway, feeling the judgment of the old, dead Glanvilles on me. What if I wasn't one of them? I didn't feel like a lady of the manor. I stared at each of the pictures; none of them really looked like anyone in the family. They looked like old-fashioned portraits, not real people.

I saw a hint of my mother's brow in one or two, but I couldn't see any features that matched mine.

I found myself outside the library again. I took deep breaths. I wasn't sure what I was going to say, but if there were more photos, my father would know where to find them.

I knocked on the old oak door, gently. No answer came.

"Daddy?"

Silence.

I swallowed and knocked again, thinking of the night before, finding my mother motionless in bed. Still no answer. I eased it open, dread clenching my throat.

My father slumped on the leather sofa in the center of the room. A globe was open, the northern hemisphere hinged back, the empty core filled with bottles. One sat on the table, a little amber liquid left at the bottom. An empty glass lay on its side next to it.

My father's head was tilted back, his eyes half-open and glassy. His phone was in his hand, facing up. He'd probably been trying to call for help. But as ever, there was no reception.

"Daddy?"

"Charlotte." He slurred so much it sounded like "Tharlotte," and my stomach tightened to see my sensible father like this. "I'm so, so sorry."

"It's not your fault."

He shook his head. "I thought she was going to make it. We were so close. I …" He shook his head. "I just wanted us to be okay. Was that too much to ask?"

His eyes were drooping.

"You need to rest."

He gave a horrible, gasping sob, and covered his eyes with his hand. I patted him, awkwardly. I'd never seen him like this and wasn't sure how to handle it.

"When did you last sleep?"

He shrugged and leaned back on the sofa. I wandered over to the bookcases. No doubt some of these could tell me more about the Lady of Levay, but it was me that I needed to research now.

"Daddy. Can I see some more family pictures? Do we have an album or something?"

He didn't answer. His eyes had closed, his head lolling back. I pulled his feet up and rolled him into a comfortable position on his side. He grunted but didn't wake.

My gaze fell on his phone. It had fallen out of his hand when I moved him, and now it lay next to him on the sofa. There had to be photos in there.

I picked it up, and I pressed the home button. It was locked, of course. I didn't know the code. I glanced back at Daddy, passed out on the sofa.

It was wrong, obviously, but I had to know.

I crawled over, as quietly as I could. I held the phone under his limp hand and lifted it up carefully, angling it so his thumb touched the home button gently, hoping the pressure wouldn't wake him. He stayed still, and when I lowered the phone again, it was unlocked.

I crept away from him before I opened the photo app.

The first photo appeared on the screen and my heart soared. It was of me, real me, the Charlotte I saw in the mirror. I exhaled, until I realized I remembered this one being taken.

The scar on my cheek was still covered by a bandage in the photo, so it couldn't have been long after I'd come home from the hospital. There were a few more of me before that one, all post-accident. I flicked back in time through the images.

Next came a series of photos of the basement. There was a dark archway in the background, water pooling on the ground in front of it. This was obviously what he'd been doing down in the basement each high tide. The water levels were a little different in each photo, some higher, some lower. The phone was in the same place. It looked like he'd set it on a stand to take timed photos.

It was obviously my father's attempt to record the flooding and the progression of structural issues in the manor's cellar or something else dull like that. I flipped through those quickly, until something caught my eye.

The picture was just like the others: the same patch of the basement, the same water pooling. I almost didn't spot the difference, but my thumb hovered over the picture, instead of swiping on to the next one. It took me a moment to realize what it was that had grabbed my attention.

She was there: The Lady of Levay.

She was caught in the image, a misty apparition in the darkened archway in the background. Daddy probably hadn't even realized there was anything other than the flooding in the picture. She was small, but it was high-resolution, and I zoomed in.

I gazed at her face, at her beautiful, careless features, wanting to lose myself in them. There was something about her that made you feel like you could let go of everything. I didn't want to click past her, but I made my finger move.

There were more pictures of the basement before that one, the water level rising and falling, but without the Lady. I fought the urge to return to the photo of her, and dwell on it, but I had to focus.

Photos taken outside the house came before that one. They were of what looked like a costumed reenactment: a battle, with people dressed just like they had been in the mist. Judging by the changes in the island's trees, these were taken in early spring. Then there was a picture not from the island. A picture of a girl perched high on a horse, and my heart stopped. She had a dark bob, my clothes and her chin held high.

It wasn't me. It was the other Charlotte.

The real Charlotte. I could see my mother in her cheekbones. She had my father's eyes. They weren't my parents at all. It was so horribly obvious that this girl belonged in my family. I was the cuckoo; she was the real child.

My breath stuck in my throat as my world crashed down around me.

I hurried back over to my father, wishing I'd never looked at his phone, wishing I'd never seen the pictures of the other Charlotte. I slid it back in his hand, and as soon as it touched his skin, his eyes opened.

Uncharacteristic fury appeared in his face. He sat up, clutching his phone.

"What are you doing?"

I couldn't answer. I barely recognized this man. I'd never seen him angry before. His whole face was distorted. He stood up. I froze as he towered over me.

He raised his free hand and slapped me across the face, hard.

Tears sprung into my eyes at the hot shock of the hit, as much as the pain. I stumbled back, clutching my cheek.

He seemed possessed. He took another step toward me as I cowered.

"I … you were asleep. I was worried. I was just checking on you." The lie came too easily to me. Is that how I'd tricked him into thinking I was his daughter? His face cleared, as if my voice woke him up properly, as if he was turning back into the man I knew. He looked at me as if he hadn't known I was there before.

"Charlotte," he said. I flinched back.

He covered his mouth. "Oh, my sweet girl. I'm so sorry. I have no idea what …" He shook his head. He looked completely confused. "I don't know what happened."

"It's okay," I said, sick with guilt, but relieved to have him back. "It's fine."

"I'm so sorry." He reached a hand toward my cheek.

It hadn't been like him. It felt like another man had loomed over me, as if Dad had been possessed.

"It's okay," I said again.

He leaned forward and hugged me. "Oh Charlotte. What just happened? I think I must have been having a nightmare."

"That makes sense. That wasn't like you."

He clutched me tighter. "You're right. That wasn't like me at all. I wouldn't do that. I'm not like that." The lights faded for a moment, before flickering back to full brightness.

"It's okay. It's okay. I think you just need to rest."

"I … You're probably right. Oh, my sweet girl. I'm so lucky to have you."

I breathed in the comforting smell of him, glad to have my normal father back again. Except he wasn't my father. He was Charlotte's father.

I clutched him tighter.

He returned my hug, then broke free of my grasp. "You're right. I should get some rest."

I let him go, reluctantly. I watched him leave the library, wishing I was his real daughter. Wishing I deserved the hug, and not the slap. Shame washed over me like oil, slick and gross. Perhaps, like my mother, on some level, he knew I wasn't his child. Perhaps that's why he'd hit me: instinctively.

How had I taken the real Charlotte's place? What had I done? And if I wasn't Charlotte, who was I?

There was one obvious answer, but it didn't make any sense.

# CHAPTER TWENTY-EIGHT

## AJAY

It was late when I woke, in the warm, red room. Grief hit me like a lorry, taking my breath.

I rolled onto my side, regret smacking into me; my uselessness with Meera and Oleander colliding.

Oleander had been going through so much; her dad's suicide and that naked photo. I should have known something was seriously wrong the last time I saw her. I shouldn't have been such a useless, infatuated idiot. I should have asked her more about the island. I should have stopped her going. I could understand her better now, but it was too late. I could see why she wanted to forget so badly.

I did too.

I didn't want to think about her skeletal hand in the cave. I didn't want that seared in my brain and all the grief and shame that came with it. Barf rose in my throat, and I swallowed it down.

Charlotte was grieving too. She'd lost her mother to whatever the hell was happening here. And she was in danger, trapped in a messed-up situation on a weird island. We all were.

I didn't want to dwell on how rubbish I'd been at helping Oleander, or my thoughtlessness with Meera. It was too bloody painful. I wanted something to do. A way to fix things, to save Charlotte, at least.

I sat up, trying to come up with a plan, any plan.

I found myself staring at the wardrobe, and it took me a moment to realize why.

The door was open slightly. Just an inch or so. But before, when I'd opened it that much, all those shoes had fallen out.

I shuffled out of bed. I noticed I was still wearing my clothes. And yes, there was a piece missing in my memories. We'd found Charlotte's mother, but that's where they stopped.

I shook my head and focused on the wardrobe. I opened the door further, carefully.

There were no shoes. Someone had taken them out of the wardrobe. Probably Charlotte's father.

But why now, with everything else going on?

I slumped back down on the side of the bed and ran a hand through my hair, trying to put things together. I looked around the rest of the room, scanning for clues as to what might have happened in my missing time, or something we could use to fight the Lady or get off the island. My gaze fell on something familiar in the bookcase in the corner.

Most of the books were old, which made sense. Charlotte said this part of the house was sometimes open to the public. They weren't exactly going to stock it with the latest blockbusters. There were leather-bound books that had one-name authors like Cicero and Herodotus.

But one of them, right in the corner of the bookcase, was newer, with a green spine.

I wandered over and pulled it out. *A History of Levay.*

I flipped to the index and started re-reading everything about the Lady of Levay, paying more attention this time, now that I knew she was real.

It took me an hour or so to work through the information about her. Without Oleander's notes to distract me, or problems keeping the island in my mind, I spotted a pattern I'd missed before: destruction. A painting ripped, carvings smashed and a monastery burned down, as well as the beheaded pre-Christian statues that archeologists had found. The more I read, the clearer it seemed. All the images of the Lady of Levay had been destroyed. Someone hadn't wanted people to see what she looked like.

I tried to remember her, but the image wouldn't form in my mind. She was beautiful, but I couldn't remember anything about her features. I couldn't even remember how old she looked. My mind slid off her, like it had off the island before I got there.

That made sense. She was a goddess of forgetting.

I could feel the edge of it then, what this whole thing was about. No one was meant to remember her. The statues and the painting were memories, in a way, memories made physical. Memories of the Goddess of Forgetting.

She wanted them destroyed.

That was probably why the monks died. Why the pre-Christian civilization perished, and why Captain Granger drowned. Lethe had to be forgotten, and she would destroy anything that stood in her way.

Which, I suspected, was us.

As I was flipping through the last pages of the book, something caught my eye. Clearly my unconscious brain was working much faster than my conscious mind, as it took me a proper read-through of the acknowledgements before I realized what I'd spotted.

A name: Peter Glanville — Charlotte's father.

*Special mention must go to my good friend Peter Glanville, who guided me so generously through the history of his home. Thank you, Peter. I particularly enjoyed some of your more interesting theories about the Lady of Levay.*

I closed the book and looked at the wardrobe again. Charlotte's father was the one who had been weird about the shoes, and now they were gone. And he was apparently an expert on the Lady of Levay.

I rubbed at my forehead. That was suspicious, right? But what the hell could a bunch of shoes have to do with any of this? Was I just getting paranoid about a middle-aged man's shoe fetish?

A knock on the door interrupted my train of thought. Charlotte was on the other side, eyes wide.

"I need you to tell me about Oleander," she said.

Nausea sloshed in my gut again as I remembered her body in the cave. I swallowed.

"What about her? Why?"

"Everything. Why did she come to Levay? What was she looking for?"

I closed my eyes for a moment and remembered what she said to me. "She wanted to forget and be forgotten. She wanted out of her life, but she didn't want to hurt anyone."

"Why? You said those were Oleander's memories, the awful ones in the mist. What happened in that garage?"

I really didn't want to go through this. But Charlotte was oddly frantic.

"That's where her father killed himself. She found him. She said the memory tortured her."

Charlotte nodded. "That's what she wanted to forget. But why did she want to be forgotten?"

"Because of the photograph."

"What photograph?"

I exhaled. "It was her boyfriend, Rupert. I didn't realize how bad things were. Tisha filled in a lot of the details after she went missing."

Charlotte settled down on the edge of the bed. "Tisha?"

"Oleander's best friend."

Charlotte gave a sad smile.

"Rupert was older, a lawyer or something. He's on bail now. There's going to be a trial."

Her eyes widened. "What did he do?"

"Shared a naked photo of her. Turns out that's child porn if someone's under eighteen."

"Bloody hell."

"He was the worst. Made out like he was in love with her, and the whole time he was living with his fiancé."

"He had a fiancé? Did Oleander know?"

"He told Oleander she was a crazy housemate, apparently. Stuff with Rupert and Ollie's dad are why …" my voice faltered. "They're why the police and everyone else thought she ran away." I wiped at my eyes, quickly. "I don't think she was trying to kill herself. I think she found out about Lethe and thought it was a chance to be forgotten. She … told me to find her if my regrets got too much."

"But you remember her? What she looks like? Everything?"

I nodded, but when I tried to bring her to mind, she wasn't quite there. "I ... think so."

"She had purple ombré hair, but what was her face like?"

"She ..." I concentrated, but I couldn't get a clear picture. I could only see the edges of her in my head: her clothes, her purple hair, not her features. Just like trying to remember the Lady.

Charlotte was staring at me, with an odd look on her face.

"Charlotte, what's this about?"

She bit her lip. "I'm not Charlotte." She looked like she was about to cry. "The girl in the mist. She was the real Charlotte. I found old pictures on Daddy's phone." She put her head in her hands. "I don't remember anything before the 'accident.' I don't know what happened to her. I just know I took over her life."

"Wait ... what?"

She looked up at me, face tear-stained. "I know. It's insane."

I tried to walk my brain through what she'd said. "The girl we saw, she was Charlotte? Then who are you?"

She stared at me for a long time, biting her lip. "Do I ... look at all familiar to you?"

I leaned back, as I finally got what this was all about. "No. You're not Oleander."

"If you can't remember what she looks like, how can you be sure?"

"Because I don't know you! Because we found Oleander's body!"

She started talking quickly. "Charlotte's father said she fell from the cliffs, when part of them collapsed. Her body could have been washed into the cave."

I shook my head, wondering if Charlotte had lost it like her mother had.

"My ... Charlotte's parents looked for her and eventually found her, injured and weak on a beach days later. But what if it wasn't Charlotte they found? What if they found Oleander, with no memories?"

"Um ... Don't you think they'd have noticed the difference between their own child and a complete stranger?"

"Mummy did, in a way."

"But not your dad? Sorry, but he doesn't seem thick to me. And you ... Charlotte fell from the cliff in May, right? Oleander didn't go missing until July."

"What if they lost time and lost their memories of Charlotte, just like you lost memories of Oleander?"

I paused. Charlotte took my silence as encouragement.

"What if they didn't remember exactly what she looked like? They were confused and heartbroken and not thinking right. They were looking for a girl on the beach, and they found one."

There was a soft tapping at the window. I jerked my head up, but it was just the patter of rain.

"Charlotte's parents were missing a daughter; I was missing a father. We'd all lost memories and needed each other so much we didn't realize we didn't fit together."

I found myself nodding for a moment before I realized how ridiculous it was. "Oleander didn't sound posh like you."

"My parents had to teach me how to speak properly again, after the accident. My ... Charlotte's mother always complained I didn't sound right."

"Oleander had purple, wavy hair."

"I straighten mine. And you said purple ombré, right? The bottom half?"

"Yes."

"Scissors exist."

"Who would have cut your hair?"

She paused, finally stumped. "I don't know."

Her hair did look a little wild today. It wasn't a huge leap to imagine that if it were long, and dyed half purple, it could look a little like Oleander's.

I derailed that train of thought. I'd know if she was Oleander, wouldn't I?

"We don't know if the visions in the mist are real," I said.

"The girl in the mist. The real Charlotte, she looked just like she did on Daddy's phone." She took a deep breath. "And that … the garage in the mist. You said that was a real memory of Oleander's, right?"

I nodded.

"I knew it was something awful. I didn't remember it, but I felt it. You said she was tortured by that memory. I almost threw myself into the sea to get away from it. That has to mean something. Some pain is deeper than memory."

I wanted to believe her so much. Because if she was right, I wasn't too late. I hadn't screwed things up. I could still save her. She looked at me with big brown eyes.

"Please, Ajay, I need to know. Am I Oleander?"

# CHAPTER TWENTY-NINE

## CHARLOTTE

Ajay stared at me for a long time, confusion in his deep brown eyes.

"I want you to be Oleander." His voice trembled. "But even if you were, you don't have her memories. How can you be her if you don't have her memories?"

I swallowed. He was right. I wasn't Charlotte, but I wasn't Oleander either. I was someone in between. I loved Charlotte's father. I couldn't remember my own.

The noise of the rain turned to a hiss as it fell harder.

Ajay looked worried. "Oleander wanted to forget and be forgotten. Were you happy here before I came?"

I didn't say anything for a long time. I couldn't face the garage I'd seen in the mist, that was clear. Oleander had chosen to leave her life behind. I had a life here. A good life, with a living, loving father.

But it wasn't my life.

"I like it here. But I don't fit. Charlotte's mother knew it. And I can't lie to my ... I mean Charlotte's father."

"He never seemed to doubt that you were Charlotte."

I bit the inside of my cheek. "What am I going to tell him? He's just lost his wife."

Ajay looked a bit awkward. "Look, um, about him. How well do you know him, if he's not your dad?"

"What do you mean?"

"Just … can you really trust him?"

A flash of anger went through me. "I know him very well. He's been wonderful. What are you even asking?"

"Sorry. I didn't mean to insult him or anything." He didn't look convinced. "But maybe we should try to find another way to get away from the island first. You can break it to him on the mainland. We —"

The crack of thunder interrupted him and brought my attention, belatedly, to the window. I hurried over and stared at the streaked glass. Rivulets of water ran down it, chasing each other. It was pouring. The trees near the house swayed wildly in the wind. Excitement bloomed through me.

"It's raining. When did it start raining?"

"A few minutes ago, I —"

I seized his hands. "It's raining! Remember what my father said? Rain might clear the mist. We have to try to get away."

"We can't take a boat out in this."

Lightning flashed, blinding me for a moment. He was right. "Yes, but we need to be ready to go as soon as the rain stops."

Ajay nodded. "Where is your … Charlotte's dad?"

"He went for a nap. I think he's in the blue bedroom. Let's go tell him."

But when we got there, the room was empty. We checked the library, the main house. I ran from room to room, growing hot with panic. We checked the other bedrooms, even the one with the woman I still thought of as my mother lying still beneath a blanket pulled up over her head. My heart pounded in my throat.

A thought hit me like a blow. "He's been acting strangely. You don't think he's gone outside, do you? Do you think Lethe could be doing something to him? Possessing him or something?"

The rain hissed at the window.

Ajay looked pale. "That might explain some things. Look, I did some reading. I think I know what she's after."

"What?"

"She wants to be forgotten. That's why she killed Captain Granger; he painted a picture of her. That's why she killed the monks; they'd carved statues of her. I think she destroys any image of herself."

Fear jolted through me like electricity. "Any image? Like ... a photo?"

"I guess. Anything that means people can remember her properly."

I felt like I was going to throw up. "My ... Charlotte's father has a photo of the Lady on his phone."

Ajay froze. "He has a photo of her on his phone? Why? How?"

"He was taking photos of the flooding in the basement. I don't think he even knows he has it. We have to find him."

Ajay looked hesitant.

"Please. He feels like my father, even if he isn't. We have to save him."

"Is there something outside he could be checking on in the storm? Do you have any pets?"

"No."

The downpour battered at the library's windows and shadows lurked between the shelves. I tried to think. The thrash of the rain mingled with the hiss of the sea outside. I ran over and peered out at what I could see of the small island, wondering if he might have gone out there in the middle of the night.

The grounds looked creepy in the soaking gloom, the stubby trees swaying with the wind, lurching out of the dark. I thought I could still see the fog in the distance, just off the coast. The rain didn't seem to be clearing it at all. The sea crept up the beach, the waves thrashing against the base of the cliffs: high tide.

With terrifying clarity, I knew exactly where he was.

"He'll be in the basement, checking on the flooding."

Ajay stared for a second. "The basement where he took the photo of her?"

I nodded, feeling like something was stuck in my throat. "Come on."

# CHAPTER THIRTY

## AJAY

Charlotte led the way.

It was easier to think of her as Charlotte, especially when she had her back to me, her dark bob swinging as she ran down the corridors of the manor. But her hair looked curlier, as if she were morphing before my eyes into Oleander.

There was something familiar about the way her arms pumped, too. Something that wasn't in her features, or her face. And there was a connection between us; there had been from the start. A connection that ran deeper than memory.

Could I have forgotten her face? Her voice? Was it that simple?

Charlotte sprinted down the curve of the main stairway, turned left down one corridor, then right through a green door into another section of the house. A plainer section. Probably the servants' areas or something.

She stopped at a wooden door. "Here," she said and opened it.

Steps led down into the dark. A wire trailed down the white-painted bricks of the wall, and Charlotte flipped a switch. A single bare lightbulb flickered into life halfway down, illuminating a narrow stone staircase, descending into mist. It was super creepy. I wasn't sure we could trust her dad, and we certainly couldn't trust the Lady.

Charlotte hesitated. "I'm not normally allowed down because of the flooding."

"I'll go first," I said.

She shook her head. "He's my … well, he feels like my father."

Man, this whole thing was so messed up.

She went down the stairs. I followed and the mist surrounded us. The lightbulb didn't help. It just turned the fog white.

"You don't have to come," she said. "I'm not sure how safe it is. Daddy was always worried about the structural integrity."

At the bottom of the stairs, I reached for her hand. She let me take it, a soft smile on her face. Something inside me sparked in response. Something warm that rushed through me. Something I hadn't felt in months.

"I'm not letting you go alone, Oleander."

"Oleander," she repeated softly.

We were so close in that suspended moment, surrounded by the soft white fog.

She went up on tiptoes and pressed her lips against mine. I'd wanted to kiss her from the first time I'd met her at the shop. It was hard to pull away, but I had to.

Hurt shone in her eyes. "I … I thought you liked me."

I swallowed down the tightness in my throat. "Yes, but you don't know what the real you wants. I don't either. Oleander told me to leave her alone, then she told me to find her. You don't remember, and I can't take advantage of that."

I felt bad, but although she looked disappointed, she nodded.

"I need to get to Daddy, anyway."

The fog was thick. I couldn't see three feet ahead. The light faded as we got further from the stairs, until the dark and the mist combined, hiding everything. I walked with one hand in front of me, the other tightly holding Oleander's.

I heard a voice, off to the left. I turned that way and saw a bit of less-dark gray mist. We blundered toward the weak sound and light. I scraped against a wall, taking the skin from the already-raw knuckles on my right hand. I kept my reaction to a sharp intake of breath, but Oleander stopped.

"It's okay," I whispered, and we crept on again.

There was definitely a faint light ahead. It was arch-shaped, so I guessed it was coming through a cellar doorway. The voice came again too. It sounded like Charlotte's dad, but after all the hallucinations, I wasn't sure. I couldn't tell what he was saying.

The mist thinned as we crept on. The light grew, and I could see Oleander again. The fog hadn't gone completely, it was just this slight blur, except at our feet, where it gathered like dry ice in a cheesy haunted house.

I'd been expecting the mist and the dark to hide us, to let us sneak up on whatever was happening and figure out how much of a part Charlotte's father had in it. But that wasn't going to work.

We got to the doorway. There were bricks lying around and stacked to one side. A few were still attached to the archway. It looked like it had been sealed up but reopened recently. Perhaps by Charlotte's father, as he was checking on the flooding.

There were steps, leading down. They weren't like the cellar stairs. These looked like they'd been carved into the ground itself. There were no wires, no light switch here, but still, light was coming from below and we headed for it, taking the steps carefully, to a corridor at the bottom.

This space wasn't built. It was tunneled into the bedrock of the island. It was obviously older than the manor above. It was ancient and had a weird, formal feeling to it, like a church.

We crept to another doorway and peered in together.

The archway opened into a big room, about the size of a school hall, but the ceiling was low. It was about a foot above my head at the edge of the room, rising a bit in the middle. The space was more like a cave than a basement, and what looked like empty statue bases were scattered around the room. The statue bases were what made it click, finally.

This was an ancient temple. The lost temple of Levay.

Oleander gasped and pointed. In the opposite corner stood Charlotte's father. The light was coming from the phone in his hand. Then I saw her: the Lady.

It was hard to make her out. She was insubstantial and the light from Charlotte's father's phone cut through her as much as it illuminated her. She was a ghost of a woman, a figure made of mist and water droplets.

Her beautiful face was twisted with fury.

Oleander lurched forward, but the Lady was holding still, and Charlotte's father was talking, so I took her arm gently, and held her back.

"I just want it all fixed. That shouldn't be too much to ask." He sniffed. "You understand, don't you? Someone has to. I didn't realize how bad it had got. I thought I still had time, until she ..." He paused, putting a hand over his mouth. His words were slurred, and he swayed a little. He sounded drunk.

Lethe's expression didn't alter, but her gaze moved to his phone and the light that fell on her.

As my eyes adjusted, I could see more of the room. Water pooled in the middle. I thought it was a big puddle, until I saw ripples moving slowly across it.

There was a kind of a channel cut into the ground along the far end of the room, a stream running down it and overflowing into the cave. Lethe was a water goddess, I remembered. Maybe this was her river.

It was deeper on one side of the room, where the stream disappeared into a heap of rubble, half-burying the channel. The wall there had collapsed at some point. A wide crack ran across the ceiling. It didn't look safe.

Charlotte's dad kept talking.

"I ... maybe you could take the memories of my wife. No ... that won't work. Her things are everywhere. There are records. Oh ... I was so close. The rain will have destroyed the posters, I could have just made her mother forget and ended this whole thing."

Oleander looked at me, her face scrunched up in confusion.

Charlotte's father continued. "Maybe if you just take away some of the last few days. I could tell people she was depressed. Yes, that could work." He nodded to himself. "It has to. I don't want anyone else to die."

Lethe looked like she was holding herself back. There was pent up fury in her, ready to be released. But below it was a kind of powerless despair, which didn't make sense. Wasn't she a goddess?

Her gaze flicked up to me. The anger left her. There was hope in her deep eyes. She looked from me to the phone and back again. She was trying to tell me something.

Charlotte's father kept talking, a manic edge to his voice. "Yes. We'll sort this now. The longer it goes on, the worse things get." He shook his head. "We'll have to get rid of the slap too. I can't believe I did that. I thought she was reaching for this." He held the phone. "It wasn't like me. I wouldn't do that."

Oleander took a step toward Charlotte's father, reaching out. Her shoe hit a stone, which clattered across the cave.

"Who's there?" His light swung to us. I blinked, blinded by the sudden brightness. His voice came from the shadows behind it.

"Charlotte ... what are you doing here?"

She raised a hand against the light. "I ... I'm not Charlotte. I don't think. I'm sorry." Her breath caught, and she put a hand over her mouth to stifle the sob.

"But ... how? Oh, sweetheart."

The light dropped as he ran over to us and swept Oleander up in a hug. She buried her face in his shoulder.

"I'm sorry," she said, voice muffled in his shoulder. "I'm so sorry. I didn't know."

"It's okay," he said. "It's all going to be okay. I'm fixing this."

"I didn't mean to trick you."

His arms loosened on her. He put his hand on her shoulder. "What are you talking about, Charlotte?"

They looked at each other for a long moment, then Oleander's gaze fell on the phone in his hand. She grabbed it from him. "Look."

He stiffened and tried to snatch it back. "What are you doing?"

Oleander spoke through tears. "I have to show you. What's the code?"

"Why do you need the code?"

Her words came out between sobs. "You have to see. I'm not the real Charlotte. You have photos of the real Charlotte. I'm so sorry. What's the code?"

His shoulders slumped. He let out a long breath.

Oleander continued, words half-swallowed by sobs, "I didn't mean to take her place, I don't think. I don't remember. I'm sorry."

Charlotte's father gave a sad smile and shook his head. "You didn't do anything wrong. We found each other. You can stay with me. You can be my daughter. Just give me back the phone."

I felt cold.

Oleander's sobs slowly stopped. "You ... knew?"

"We'll still be a family. We lost your mother, but there's still the two of us, right?"

She took a step back. "But ... how long have you known?"

Charlotte's father sighed. "Since I saved you. You were such a mess, so confused and heartbroken. I knew I could help. We could help each other."

Oleander looked at me, probably for reassurance, or maybe she expected me to do something. All I could do was stare at them both like a total idiot as things fell into place.

Of course he knew. That explained the shoes.

They were Charlotte's shoes. Oleander could fit Charlotte's clothes, but Charlotte had a different shoe size. For Oleander to take Charlotte's place, her father had to buy new shoes and get rid of the old ones.

Oleander turned back to Charlotte's father. "I ... I didn't steal her life?"

"No. She disappeared before you arrived. I still don't know what happened to her." There was a desolation in his eyes as he said it. "I was searching for any trace of her when I found you, washed up on the beach. It was a miracle."

They were so focused on each other, neither of them noticed Lethe take a step toward me. She pointed at the phone in Oleander's hand, eyes pleading.

"The girl I found on the shore was hysterical." He cupped her chin in his hand. "A father searching for his daughter. A daughter who lost her father. It was meant to be. We found each other. We made a family."

Oleander shook her head, clearly overwhelmed.

I felt sick. "You have a family, Oleander. Your mum's desperate to find you."

"But I … don't remember her," Oleander said.

Charlotte's father took her hand. "You were tortured by your own guilt. You wanted to leave it all behind. You wanted to forget and be forgotten, and I helped you do that. If your mother really loves you, she'd want you to be happy. And you can be happy with me."

"You're not Charlotte!" I said to Oleander. "Could you live with that? Always being the fake?"

"You wouldn't be a fake. You don't have to remember any of this. I'll fix it all. You'll never have to wonder, never have to know you were Oleander. Just give me the phone."

The anger in Lethe's eyes grew stronger. She stared at the phone in Oleander's hand.

That's when it clicked.

The photo was a solid memory of the goddess of forgetting, like Captain Granger's painting, like the abbot's statues. A memory of a goddess who should be forgotten.

It gave the holder power over Lethe.

Oleander turned to me. "How can I decide if I don't even remember being Oleander?"

"You didn't want to remember. You wanted to forget," Charlotte's father said. "I helped you get rid of your memories. You wanted a father. I was there for you."

"Is that what you still want?" I asked.

"How am I meant to decide without my memories?"

"I've told you the whole story! Give me the phone." Charlotte's father said. He sounded like he was trying to stay calm and failing. "You already decided."

Oleander looked between the two of us, clearly torn.

"You're right," I said. "You should know the whole story before you decide."

She smiled at me, then turned to Charlotte's father, face apologetic. "It's not that I don't want to be your daughter. I just want to make sure it's the right choice. Can I get my memories back, please?"

There was a change in the air, as if the whole island exhaled.

Charlotte's dad froze. He stared over my shoulder.

I turned. Lethe was smiling. She tipped her head back and lifted her arms from her sides.

A whooshing, rushing noise came. The fog that formed her grew more substantial. She raised her arms higher, and the mist got darker. It pulled from the air and the water of the cave, forming a raging, twisting darkness in front of her.

It reached toward Oleander, like a hungry animal.

"What's happening?" she said.

"You're holding the phone." Charlotte's dad yelled. "You asked for your memories back. Lethe has to do what you said! Stop her! Tell her to stop now!"

Lethe ignored him, chin high.

The fog drifted to Oleander. She backed away, trying to swat at it with her hands. She kept retreating, until her back hit the wall.

The mist cut her off from us. It coiled toward her, reaching for her face. There were images in there, hundreds, thousands of them, superimposed on each other, twisting together. I saw flashes of Oleander's mother smiling, of Tisha laughing, of me holding a shell sculpture, and of a gray office with Rupert holding out a card. They blurred into each other until they looked like waves, washing toward her.

I stared at it all, wondering how to stop this or if I should.

"Ajay!" Oleander shouted, as she disappeared into the darkness.

I ran toward her, too late.

The fog swallowed her whole.

# CHAPTER THIRTY-ONE

## OLEANDER

I was alone, in the storm and a fog so deep I couldn't see out. Charlotte's father and Ajay were on the other side. I couldn't even hear them. The hiss of the mist enveloped me, cutting me off.

I stepped forward into chaos: suffocating, head-splitting visions and noise. I stumbled back out of the mist, gasping. I took deep breaths, trying to recover from the shock, the jarring feeling of a whole world trying to force its way into my mind.

I clutched the phone tightly. I could stop this. Charlotte's father had made that clear. I controlled the goddess of forgetting. I could step back into my life as Charlotte. I could erase my doubt. I didn't need to know any of this.

Here, in the eye of the storm, the mist surrounded me at a slight distance, images churning within it, like ghosts caught in a spinning void, roiling and twisting. It reached toward me, tentatively, hungrily. I wanted to stumble away, but the wall was at my back.

Who was Oleander, really? I'd only heard Ajay's story, and Charlotte's father's. In front of me was her story — my story.

I clutched the phone tighter. I could see a little. Find out what she really thought. Let in a few memories and stop before the garage.

The mist coiled in the dark of the underground temple. A tendril crept forward. An image formed, separating from the blackness of the fog: a lost memory, tight and dark. The moment uncoiled, unspooled, unwound, until it was finally clear; a scene hanging upon the air like a projection.

A memory of a stolen boat on dark water.

My memory.

It flowed toward me, and I watched, mesmerised as it grew close, as it flowed into me.

I saw myself arrive at Levay Island, back when I was Oleander, and sink beneath the water. The memory was filled with despair and cold. It hurt. But I inhaled instinctively, letting it in. It returned to me, finding its place in my mind.

I steeled myself and began learning who I was.

Other memories followed fast from the dark, memories of meeting Rupert. They stung with shame and tasted bitter with regret. But I needed to understand.

Then came a bright memory, a light memory. There was a little shop, and Ajay, and hope and excitement. I felt it return to where it belonged, felt it knit a part of me back together again, and fill in more of the story of Ajay and me.

Now I wasn't just curious; I was hungry. I wanted more of our story. More of him.

The memories came fast after that, piling one on top of another, painful memories of losing my virginity, of a naked photo shared among my classmates.

The mist grew thicker, louder, as if impatient. It swamped me, smothering my senses. It swallowed me in its damp embrace.

It pressed in on me. Feelings and sensations, too many to process. Rooms, people, emotions. Tisha, from a few years back, laughing on swings with me at a park; my mother cradling me when I was little, fighting with me when I was older; classrooms; camp sites; theme parks. I tried to take them in, tried to understand them, but they came so fast. Some settled soft as snowflakes, others were gut-punches.

A lifetime of memories, of being Oleander. They cut off the air as they tried to force their way back in. I started choking, hacking on the damp fog as it fought to fill my lungs. I inhaled, desperately, trying to let them all in before they drowned me.

I still clutched the phone, but I couldn't speak if I tried.

The memories forced their way home. Me staining the bath purple when I dyed the bottom half of my hair and Mum lecturing me about it. Ants tickling my ankles on a school hiking trip.

Through it all, came one memory. Crueler, brighter, sharper than the others, a monster in the dark of the mist, coming for me. The nightmare I couldn't escape.

Once again, I was at my father's door, knocking to no answer. Once again, I smelled the exhaust. I stumbled away from the memory, but the wall blocked my escape. I tried to close my mind.

The memory was still there, inescapable.

The side door. The mist. The garage. The car. The body.

The memory was thicker, wetter than mere mist. It filled my senses, stuck to me, covered my face, my mouth, my nose. I wanted to call out then. Wanted to tell the goddess to stop. But I couldn't or I'd let it in.

I wasn't going to let it in. The water blocked the air, blocked my breath.

The car was the only clear thing as the world grew dark.

I couldn't control this. I couldn't pick and choose which memories to see, which to keep. They were all mine, and this was the strongest of all.

My lungs screamed at me. I was drowning again, like in the waters around Levay. I had to decide. The memory might break me. It had before.

I wanted to live. My future was on the other side, my future as Charlotte or my future as Oleander. I didn't have to hold this memory. I could ask Lethe to take it away again. I just had to let it in for now, enough to get the breath to command her. In one deep inhale, I did.

It slid in my chest like a knife.

I collapsed, folding onto the wet ground. Still the memories came. The months of heartbreak, shame and guilt that followed tore into me. The funeral. The sleepless nights. It built up in my head, a tide of grief and guilt that filled my soul, leaving no room for thought, until I was numb, until I couldn't move, until all I could do was weep, hoping to let a little of the water out, and ease the unbearable pressure.

I didn't just understand Oleander. I was her.

I'd been so arrogant to think I could survive what she could not.

# CHAPTER THIRTY-TWO

## AJAY

The mist was a wall in front of me. It hissed and seethed. I wanted to push through but was scared of hurting Oleander.

"What's happening?" I said.

"We have to save her. Get the phone!" Charlotte's dad's face was stricken with panic. "Then Lethe is yours to command, and you can fix this."

I stumbled into the mist. It twisted around me like a hurricane of memory. I tripped and fell to the ground. I tried to crawl forward, but I got turned around, and I found myself back in the temple, coughing and spluttering, the mist behind me.

Lethe looked down on me. She didn't look angry. She was assessing me.

Charlotte's father ran at the mist too, but Lethe simply raised a hand, and the water grew solid as ice. He stumbled back, bellowing in pain.

"Go back in!" he yelled at me. "She won't let me. You have to get the phone. Stop her before it's too late!"

Lethe held my gaze. Her anger was not for me.

I could get back into the mist. Maybe even get the phone. I could control her. *Yours to command,* Charlotte's father had said.

I didn't want to command anyone.

The mist was fading. I could see Oleander through it, a darker shape in the fog. She swayed. "Oleander!"

She fell to her knees.

"The Lady is killing her! Get the phone! Make her stop!" Charlotte's dad yelled.

Oleander dropped her head into her hands and crumpled, still holding the phone. She folded into herself until she lay on the ground in a ball.

The mist grew thinner. It was fading into Oleander, I realized. The memories were returning home. I ran over and knelt next to her, leaning in close.

She lay still, eyes open. For a second, I was terrified she was dead, but she blinked.

"Oleander!"

Tears slid down her cheeks.

"What have you done?" Charlotte's dad said.

I turned back. Lethe stood between him and us, blocking the way. He looked as if he were going to push past her, but she raised one hand, and I saw the fear in his eyes. He was terrified of the goddess he'd been controlling.

I turned back to my friend.

"Oleander?" I wasn't sure if she heard. I pushed her hair back off her forehead, but she didn't flinch. She was catatonic.

"I've been trying to protect her from this." Charlotte's father said. "I got Lethe to hide the island, to let no boats through, to only let people on the island remember Levay. I just needed long enough for her to settle in, long enough to clear the museum and the library of everything to do with the Lady, and then no one would ever know. I was so close before you came. I'd healed her pain, given her another chance, a new life."

He covered his face with his hands. "Then it all fell apart. My ... My wife ..." His voice caught. "Oleander is all I have left. We have each other, can't you see that? She needs me. I need her."

Lethe hovered between us. Charlotte's dad nodded at her. "Don't give her an inch. She's not a person. She's a monster. The only thing stopping her killing us all is that phone. She killed Captain Granger, after his wife destroyed the portrait of Lethe."

Anger twitched in Lethe's face at the captain's name.

Charlotte's dad continued. "She killed the abbot after one of the monks destroyed the statues. I worked it out from the legends. I knew the temple and a buried spring were below the house, and I had a theory about Lethe, but I didn't test it until Charlotte went missing."

"What happened to Charlotte?"

Charlotte's dad shook his head. "I think she jumped. She'd been kicked out of school. My wife, Eleanor, blamed herself, blamed her parenting. Eleanor had always been fragile, and ... grief and guilt are a cruel combination."

Oleander lay still. Tears ran silently down her face.

"I caught Eleanor one night with pills. I stopped her in time, but I knew she'd try again. I decided to see if my theory was true. I decided to take her grief from her. I broke down the doorway. I set up the camera on my phone and finally, I got the picture." He glanced at Lethe. "She wanted to hide, but this is my island."

I didn't like the triumph on his face.

"Make her better, make her Charlotte again. Make Lethe take her memories away."

"Why didn't you just make your wife forget Charlotte?"

He laughed. "That's exactly what I did at first. I thought Eleanor would heal. I thought she'd be okay if she didn't remember what we'd lost."

For a second, he looked ashamed. "You have to understand; I was desperate. I lost my child, and I was going to lose my wife, too."

"It didn't work?"

"Charlotte was too much for her to forget. It was … awful, watching Eleanor go from room to room, looking for something, not remembering what it was. There was a hole in our home, and we were all lost in it. It was a miracle when Oleander arrived."

There was a flicker in Oleander's eyes. I wondered if she was fully catatonic, or if she was listening. I kept talking.

"How did you make your wife believe Oleander was her daughter when she didn't even remember she was a mother?"

"I got Lethe to give back vague memories. I had everyone forget Charlotte's face. The mind is elastic. It fills in the gaps."

Charlotte's dad reached his hands out, pleading. "She was happy until you came. Then you told me about the posters. I couldn't have pictures of her stuck all over the mainland. I just had to wait for the rain to ruin the ones that were up and make Oleander's mother forget to put up new ones."

He hung his head then. "I know how that sounds. I really do. But it's for Oleander. It's all to save her from this," he gestured at her on the floor. "She nearly drowned trying to get away from her old life. She can have a happy one here as Charlotte. Her mother would agree if she knew."

Oleander obviously hadn't told Charlotte's dad about the on-line photograph that rain wouldn't wash away. But if she were Charlotte, no one would work it out. It was a fuzzy picture, Tisha had said. Without her name, without her purple hair, Oleander could be free of it.

The agony was etched into Oleander's face. It hurt to see her like that. I did want to take it away, just like Charlotte's dad had. The last of the mist was fading, sinking into her. She had her memories back.

Oleander's mum had been heartbroken. But would she want her daughter to be happy, even if it meant she never saw her again? I wanted Oleander back. But that was selfish.

There were no happy endings here, for any of us. There was just the right thing for Oleander. But what was it?

Her hand was still tight on the phone, knuckles white.

That's when I realized. It was all so simple. There was no right decision for me to make. The decision wasn't mine.

"Get it now!" Charlotte's father said.

I stood up and faced him, calmly. "No. She wanted her memories. She wanted to decide. This is Oleander's choice."

# CHAPTER THIRTY-THREE

## OLEANDER

Oleander was in the water, struggling for the island, losing the fight, sinking under the waves. The water closed over her head, sealing her there, away from the air, away from her own life. Or what was left of it.

It churned around her, but there was a stillness here. There was a final forgetting if she chose it. Pressure built in her lungs. She could let it out, she could inhale the water. It would hurt so much, but it would soon be over. She'd be gone. All that would be left of her would be memory. They'd assume she killed herself. Her father's death showed it ran in the family, and the naked photo was the trigger.

Those things would define her. They would be what everyone remembered; the decisions that other people — her father and Rupert — made for her.

She doesn't want to be remembered that way: the tragic girl, the cautionary tale.

But what does she have to live for? What is it she wants? She's barely thought about that in so long. Her life has all been about what others wanted from her: her father, and then Rupert.

She knows what she doesn't want. She doesn't want to be controlled by a photograph. A naked picture doesn't seem important here, in the breathless black. It's humiliating, but it's not worth dying over.

She doesn't want Rupert. She doesn't want to spend her life trying to make him happy, trying to keep him from hurting himself. She tried that with her father, and she failed. That's clear too. She wonders why she couldn't see that before.

And in the dying dark she realizes Rupert never needed her anyway. He used the photo to make her stay with him. He probably used his threats of self-harm the same way. It was all a scam, and it's one she can walk away from. He never really had power over her. She should have left him a long time ago.

She wants to be able to make her own choices. She wants to be herself again. She wants to keep her purple hair. She wants to eat chips on the floor of a gift shop, not dinners in fancy restaurants where she always felt out of place. She wants to laugh and joke and relax again.

She wants Ajay.

He made her laugh. He never tried to control her. He was happy with her friendship when that was all she had to offer. He never demanded things from her, like her father and Rupert. Maybe her friendship was all he wanted, but what she really wants is to find out.

She swims for the surface. Hard. It's further than she thought; she's been tumbled by the waves. She struggles, fighting the dark, the pain in her lungs, the ache, the need to breathe. She kicks and flails and throws everything she has left at it.

She breaks the surface, barely. She's not clear of the waves when she has to inhale, and she sucks in sea spray along with air.

She chokes, trying to clear the saltwater from her lungs, letting more in. Waves hit her, filling her nose, her throat. She's kicking and coughing and struggling for her life.

But the tide is carrying her to the beach, and not the rocks. She's drowning still, when the waves push her onto the island. There's water in her lungs. She finds sand under her hands, crawls a little and coughs up some of the sea. She vomits, then drags herself a little further, until the waves are weak, and all but her feet are clear of them.

She collapses onto her side and unconsciousness takes her.

When she wakes, she's being carried. Suspended between two arms. She looks up into an unfamiliar face, a man's face, her father's age.

"Hold on," he whispers to her. "Hold on."

She wakes in a bed in a red room. The same man is by her as she stirs.

"You're awake."

She nods. She's stiff, and she wonders how long she's been unconscious.

"Can you talk?"

She finds she can, although her voice is weak. He has a lot of questions. She tells him she wants to go home, asks him to call her mum. He takes down the number and tells her help is on the way. He brings her soup and helps her drink it. He asks her about why she left, how she got to the island. She tells him everything, and he listens closely. When he leaves, she sleeps again.

She wakes later, jolting upright into something sharp, something that cuts into her face. She cries out. He's holding scissors and a handful of purple hair.

"Lie still!" he says, and his face is different, furious. "That's your fault! That wouldn't have happened if you hadn't moved!"

The pain is shocking. She puts a hand to her cheek, and it comes back wet with blood. The line on her face where he cut her is hot agony.

"Lie still!" he shouts again. His anger and the scissors in his hand scare her into submission. Blood seeps though her fingers. He grabs her hair, roughly, and slices off the purple ends. "This is for your own good."

He strides from the room, taking bright handfuls of her hair with him. She stares at the door as he leaves, still holding her face, trying to breathe through the pain, trying to work out what to do, but she's too weak to run, and this is an island.

The man comes back, full of apologies. He promises her it will be okay. He brings a first aid kit and tends to her cheek. He carries on cutting her hair until it's a neat bob. This time, she's too scared to move. When he leaves, she tries to think of a way to escape.

Then the Lady appears beside her bed, and her worries lift.

# CHAPTER THIRTY-FOUR

## OLEANDER

It was all there. The whole thing. My life as Oleander and Charlotte, complete. How I'd let Charlotte's father shape me into his perfect daughter. He'd shaped himself into a perfect father too — a calm, loving father — by making me forget anything else.

I never remembered him losing his temper. He made sure of that.

I'd woken with bruises I couldn't explain. I'd woken with time missing. He'd comforted me, blamed the accident, blamed my head injury. I believed him and stopped trusting myself, just as I had with Rupert. Bit by bit, I put all my faith in him. Bit by bit, I became his version of Charlotte.

It was more than I could take: a head full of fractured memories of two different people. The memory of my father's death was fresh and raw, cutting into me as if it were new. With it came the guilt that had sent me to Levay, the guilt that had almost killed me.

But I didn't have to face it alone.

I wasn't just Oleander anymore. I had my memories of being Charlotte, too. I had her perspective. When I was Charlotte, I'd known Oleander's father's death wasn't her fault. It was obvious from the outside.

Part of me had always known this. Mum and Tisha had told me. Ajay had told me. I hadn't let myself believe it. But when I was Charlotte, I *felt* it. I'd forgiven myself so easily when I'd been someone else.

All I'd really needed was my own forgiveness. Now I had it. I held it tight, a light against the fog of the garage.

The man I'd thought was my father stood in front of Ajay, ranting and raving. They seemed so far away, and I couldn't move yet. My mind was still fractured.

I remembered going to see Ajay the night we survived the cave. I'd crept to the Red Room to see if he was okay once I'd finished my bath and sorted my hair, carrying the stone I'd found in the cave. He was there with the man I'd thought was my father.

Ajay sat up straight in bed and called me Oleander.

I'd been confused, shaken by his certainty. Charlotte's father had dismissed it as the ravings of a boy who'd spent too long in the water until Ajay stumbled out of the bed and pulled a poster with my face on it from his jacket pocket.

Charlotte's father lost it. He snatched the poster out of Ajay's hands and threw it on the fire. He called him a liar, and yelled at me, shoving me from the room so hard I dropped the stone from the cave. He slapped me when I asked what was happening. He dragged me back into my room and told me to stay there.

Hurt and bewildered, I did what he said, sitting on my bed, shaking, until the Lady came to take the memories from me.

I felt violated. He'd tricked me into caring for him. He'd stolen my guilt about my real father, corrupted it, and repackaged it as love.

But I had the power. I had the phone. I had my memories and my own forgiveness.

Ajay came toward me, the one thing that had made sense in both my lives. Charlotte's father shouted at him, demanding he take the phone. I clutched it tighter. No one was taking it from me. I'd never let anyone make me do anything I didn't want ever again.

Not even Ajay.

I had the power now. I'd take them both down if I had to.

But Ajay didn't reach for the phone. He faced Charlotte's father instead, standing up for me, for my choices. Warmth flooded me. I'd been right about him.

Lethe's attention turned to me. She was so beautiful. Understanding flowed between us, wordlessly. In that space, we were equals. She'd been controlled by a photograph too. There was no shame in it, if a goddess could be snared the same way.

I knew what I had to do, for us. I held her gaze as I raised the phone above my head and brought it down on a rock.

It shattered in my hand.

# CHAPTER THIRTY-FIVE

## AJAY

Charlotte's dad ran at Oleander, but I was in the way. I leapt at him, and he stumbled and fell. He shoved me off and scrambled to his feet, but he was too late.

The phone shattered. Without the bright screen, the basement plunged into darkness.

Light came back, a gentle, warm illumination, held by Lethe. A memory of light, clutched in her hand: candles and torches and bonfires on the beach swirling within. She leaned back and exhaled, closing her eyes as if to savor the moment.

"What have you done?" Charlotte's dad demanded. "You stupid boy!"

He flung himself at me.

I barely got my arms up before the blows came. "You … should … have … taken … the … phone." His punches came down on my forearms, hard, then right in my stomach. He put his whole weight behind his fists. Pain blocked out all thought. I fought for breath, pathetically unable to defend myself.

"Get off him!"

A pause in the attack. Oleander had managed to get on his

back with an arm around his neck. But he was way too strong for her, twisting from her grip and turning his fury on her.

I ran at him, taking a swing, but my punch was pathetic. He pushed me down easily and I fell hard on the stone ground, still winded. I wasn't a fighter at the best of times, and I was still way too weak after everything.

Still, no one said I had to fight fair.

I looked around desperately for something to even the odds. Oleander had got away from him, but he advanced on her as she backed toward a corner. The room had grown misty, but through the fog I saw the box of Charlotte's old things. I grabbed a laptop, the heaviest thing I could spot. I ran over and swung it at his head, hard. It connected with a dull thud, and he reeled backward toward the steps, swearing.

Oleander hurried toward me. "We have to get out of here."

She was right, but Charlotte's father was in front of the exit. He'd recovered from the blow and stood in a fighting stance.

Then the Lady drifted between us and him.

In her hands, the mist coalesced and formed an image: Charlotte. It was the real Charlotte, the one we'd seen before, but a few years younger. Charlotte's father froze, staring at the image. In it, his daughter flinched, arm raised protectively.

"No!" A blow came down; an arm in a shirt, striking her across the side of her head.

Through the fog, Charlotte's father shook his head. "That never happened."

He took a swing at the Lady, but she faded into the mist surrounding her, and another image of the real Charlotte appeared to our right. She was a lot younger, and she was holding an ice-pack to her face. Her father stood above her.

"It was an accident, okay? That's what we're going to tell your mother. You shouldn't have wound me up like that, but I forgive you."

Charlotte nodded, mutely.

"She's making it up!" Charlotte's dad shouted.

That's when I realized. He hadn't just been taking memories from us. He'd had Lethe remove some of his own, the things he didn't want to remember about himself.

"She's trying to distract me!" He swatted the memory out of the way and advanced on us again, hands forming into fists. "You … why couldn't you just let things be? I'd almost fixed them all!"

I grabbed Oleander's hand, and we backed up. In front of us, another vision appeared, halting him: Charlotte's mum.

"You must see there's something wrong with her. She isn't herself. She doesn't even sound like herself."

"Don't say that." There was a warning growl in Charlotte's dad's reply in the memory. Her mother took a step back, the ice in her drink clinking against the glass.

"You have to be nice to her."

"I … It's just …" There was a plea in her eyes, fear balanced against the need to explain, the need to deal with something wrong at the heart of her world. "You must see it, Peter. You must."

He didn't hit her in the memory. He barely raised his hand. But she stumbled back with a whimper, unsteady, perhaps because of the alcohol she clutched. Her heel caught on a book on the ground, and she fell hard. Her head hit the corner of a solid mahogany desk with a crack that made me wince.

"It was an accident!" the real Charlotte's dad said. "We were just talking. She fell! You can't blame me for wanting to forget that!"

He leaned down and grabbed a rock from the ground. He threw it at the scene, but it went straight through the mist.

The Lady of Levay raised one arm, dark triumph in her eyes. More images spun around her, faint in the light she held. There weren't as many, which made sense. Oleander had her whole life taken from her. Charlotte's father had carefully chosen what he wanted to forget, curating his own memories.

I knew what was coming next. I'd seen it out at sea, twice. Lethe had been trying to show me the truth from the start.

There she was: Charlotte. The real Charlotte. She was furious, swearing in her posh voice. Her voice that obviously fitted the manor so much better than Oleander did.

"Where do you think I got my temper from? Pack me off to any school you want, but I'm never going to be some perfect little girl. You know why? Because I was raised by you."

She didn't look afraid of him, like her mother did. Maybe she'd underestimated his fury. Maybe she no longer cared.

In the memory, a hand swung from the side and connected with her face.

She stumbled back, shocked and furious. Another punch came, and another. I couldn't watch. I turned away, but I could hear her dad grunt with the force he put in his fists, and I heard her react in soft gasps, in too much pain and shock to cry out.

The blows kept coming, until I couldn't hear Charlotte again. I opened my eyes, and the image hung on the air. Charlotte lying still, eyes open, a little blood in her mouth.

He'd killed her. He'd beaten his own daughter to death.

"No!" He grabbed another stone from the ground. "It's all lies!"

I don't think he believed himself.

I thought he was going to go for the Lady again, so I wasn't prepared when he ran at me, rock raised high. I didn't have time to react as he swung it toward my skull. But Oleander was there, shoving him backward, catching him off balance as he lunged in for the blow.

He stumbled back, right into the mist of memories. It was thicker now, a swirling mass of images. He yelled, punching the air around him, trying to pummel the visions into submission. They tightened around him like a noose. The mist was more solid now, and Charlotte's father struggled to get out of it.

In the Lady's hands, another ghostly image appeared: a clifftop. Charlotte's body. Her dad wept, muttering apologies she would never hear. He rolled her off the edge and into the sea below. The memory joined the others surrounding him.

In reality, he was frantic, screaming and swearing as the images drew closer. Then suddenly he went quiet, closing his mouth tightly, like he was holding his breath.

Lethe's face was stone as he writhed and swatted. Still the memories flowed from her hands to thicken the mist around him.

Another image: him raging at us this time, Oleander and me, in the room with Charlotte's mum lying dead in front of us. He was screaming at us for trying to escape the island as we stood together, frozen in the face of his fury.

In the temple, Oleander grabbed onto my arm. "Let the memories in!" she shouted at her fake dad. "Don't fight them!"

He flailed at the fog, choking.

Oleander's grip on my arm tightened until it was painful. "Let them in!"

His jaw was set, his mouth shut. The mist condensed into water as he punched at it. His eyes were bulging. He was drowning in memories.

Oleander turned to Lethe. "Make him let them in."

The goddess pointed at Peter Glanville. I knew what she meant. It was his choice. He could let the memories in and live. He could block them out and die.

I knew what he was going to choose.

All his pretense was gone, and he was his true self, angry and out of control. He swung at the images, punched at the things he'd done, the things he refused to remember.

His eyes, distorted through the water, were growing red. He fell to his knees.

I took Oleander's arms and gently turned her around, away from the horror. "You can't help him."

"He's going to die!"

I pulled her to me. "That's his choice."

He slumped onto the ground, still struggling. The watery mist covered him, an unnatural mound of liquid, thick with memory, rippling with each of his weak punches.

As he moved less, so did the water.

Oleander buried her head in my shoulder. I held her there for a long time, shaking and sobbing against me as her fake dad drowned in his own memories.

Finally, he was still, eyes open and staring, mouth set in a sneer of defiance.

The water around him turned back into mist and drifted to Lethe. She opened her arms to receive it, to welcome his lost memories, the memories of the dead.

But it didn't stop there. More mist flowed from his prone body. It coiled out, reaching toward the Lady as if reaching for home, and I saw other images in there: a bride, obviously Charlotte's mum when she was young, turning to face him, eyes alight; a toddler, taking small, shaky steps toward his outstretched arms; and him running up a beach, a girl with purple hair unconscious in his arms. Those were the memories he'd chosen to keep. The memories he'd tried to build himself out of.

"We have to go," Oleander said, as the last of the memories left the dead man.

She wasn't looking at him. She was looking at Lethe. There was something passing between them, an understanding I was totally shut out of.

A soft hiss grew in the room. It took me a moment to figure out where it was coming from: the water channel. The pool was growing, inching across the floor of the weird cave-temple. It rose, slowly. It reached Charlotte's father's body, and began to flow around him, over him.

"Yeah. I think you're right."

Together, we hurried out of the temple and up the stairs. As we climbed, the single light bulb went out. I glanced down to the basement one last time as we reached the top. Water lapped at the bottom step. Waves were forming, rising and falling in the light of memory that still shone from Lethe.

We ran into the main house. "Keep going," I said, thinking of the crack that reached across the basement ceiling. We sprinted to the main entrance. There was a groaning noise from all around us. We ran faster, desperately, across the tiled floor, to the main doors.

Oleander yanked the nearest one open, and we piled out into the rain. We stumbled downhill from there, sprinting toward the beach we'd both washed up on. Only when we were a good distance from the house did we stop and turn.

It happened slowly, then all at once. A chunk of the hillside between the manor and the cliffs collapsed into itself. The gush of water washed away the rubble, briefly revealing the cave we'd found, the cave we'd survived in, close to the house. The water pushed the rubble toward the cliffs, scouring the hillside.

The landslide undermined the manor. One side of the house leaned in. It balanced there for a long moment, in defiance of gravity. Then it folded into the rest of the house with a rumble like thunder.

The roof followed, bending and sinking into the building. The other walls tipped and fell, the manor crumbling in on itself, until it was a mess of bricks and chimneys. Water pooled in the ruins, seeping around the rubble, mixing with mud and the weak hillside, forming a slurry that began to heave toward the cliffs.

It picked up speed, tumbling away from us, following the path the water had gouged over the edge of the cliffs. It spilled over, the whole mess collapsing into the sea and burying the mouth of the cave below.

It took a while for the rumble and hiss to die down.

"She demolished it," I said, once the shock had faded. "All of it."

Oleander nodded. "It was used to control her: the temple, the monastery, the manor. Her stream runs through it all, but now no one can reach it."

"Why didn't she do that before?"

Oleander gave a little laugh. "That's always the question, isn't it? Not 'why did people try to control her?' Maybe she wanted to trust people, to give us a chance." She stared at the remains of the hillside. "And sometimes you just don't realize how much power you have until you use it."

I wondered if Lethe had been the one to collapse the fallen wall we'd seen in the cellar, trying to hide her temple-cave many years ago. I wondered if the captain's wife had bricked up the archway that Charlotte's father had broken through. Maybe Lethe had thought that would be enough.

"She sent me to save you when you were drowning. She sent the voices in the cave," Oleander said. "She used those ancient memories to show us the way, to save our lives. She woke me at low tide."

Oleander and I watched as mist coiled out of the mess of the house. Lethe formed in its swirls. She strode toward the shore, smiling and nodding as she passed, as if inviting us to follow.

We did.

Ahead of Lethe, the edge of dawn was visible through the fog. Lethe raised her arms, and brought them down, hard.

A wave crashed out from the shore. It pushed out to sea, and as it flowed, the mist retreated, revealing the peaks and valleys of the wild waves, gray after the storm.

The fog billowed away over the sea and to the mainland beyond.

# CHAPTER THIRTY-SIX

## OLEANDER

On the mainland, memories drift back to their owners in the dark: faint swirls of mist. They slide into their dreams; recollections of trips to a manor on an island; days spent on the beach; the cool of the wind on the ferry trip over.

An early dog-walker inhales, and the scent on the air reminds him of a reenactment he took part in, a civil war battle recreated on Levay Island. Strange, how he hadn't thought of it in a while.

A teenager turns over in her bed, dreaming of a secret kiss behind the manor on a school trip. She smiles but does not wake.

A woman, unable to sleep in months, remembers Levay. The island comes back to her like an intake of breath in her dim bedroom. She sits up, heart racing. In seconds, she's in her daughter's room staring at the photographs stuck to the wall. It's so obvious. She wonders why she never thought of looking there.

She has to get to Levay.

She dashes for her phone to call the parents of the boy who helped her put up posters. The boy to whom she owed a huge apology.

The boy who went missing a few days later.

# CHAPTER THIRTY-SEVEN

## OLEANDER

The sun rose, revealing clear skies and wide horizons. Gulls called out, flying in from the sea, bringing their familiar screech and chatter with them.

Ajay kept hold of my hand and I squeezed his, reveling in his touch, drinking in the light, the pink of the early sunrise. The sky shone brighter than I remembered as it rose, blue and metallic bright, sharper than I'd seen in months.

Lethe nodded, satisfaction in her face, then she turned to Ajay and lifted a hand.

It was a small memory that drifted toward him. I saw my face in it, saw him smile as it slipped back into its proper place.

"It's you," Ajay said. "I mean, I knew that. But now I remember. You are Oleander. It's really you."

His expression was bright, but Lethe was looking at me. We stood there, for a long moment, a goddess and a girl, joined in our shared understanding of what it felt like to be controlled.

She mimed something, pulling, drawing something out with her hands. She pointed at my head.

"What's she saying?" Ajay asked.

"I think … I think she's offering to take a memory from me. To let me forget."

Lethe nodded.

"I think it's to thank me for freeing her."

"The car, your father. You can get rid of that memory," Ajay said.

Lethe held her hand out, palm up, like an invitation to give her the memory, as if it could be handed over as easily as a stone. Which I supposed, for Lethe, it could be.

I stared at her for a long moment, into the careless ease of her face. I was tempted. The memory hurt. It still took my breath.

Eventually I swallowed. I shook my head. "I can't … I want to, so much. But that's what he did, Charlotte's father. He got rid of the memories of when he was to blame. I can't be like him."

"But it wasn't your fault," Ajay said. "You're not like Charlotte's dad at all."

"I know. But if I give this away, I don't think I'll ever fully believe that. I don't think I'll ever heal right. I have to work through this."

He squeezed my hand.

"And I know what happens when you try to cut the memories out. I lost control of my life. They're mine to carry. I have to work out how to do that without them hurting me."

Lethe nodded, as if I'd said the right thing, but she wasn't done. She turned to Ajay, hand open. She wasn't offering to take a memory this time. There was something already in her palm, something that coiled and twisted. He glanced at me, and we both leaned in to see.

It unfolded, opened. An everyday forgotten memory. It looked like a waiting room. A name was called, but I didn't catch it. A middle-aged woman coughed right into her hands, then stood, clutching the arms of the chairs to push herself up to standing. Gross.

She passed a mother with a young girl who came in through another door. They had the same shade of skin, the same warm eyes as Ajay, who leaned in closer to watch as they appeared. The mother and daughter made a beeline for the woman's chair and the empty one next to it. The little girl climbed into the now-empty seat, clutching the arms, and smiling at her mother.

The memory faded, folding into itself. I shook my head, baffled. She smiled at my confusion and nodded at Ajay.

His mouth was open. He stared at the space where the image had been.

"That was our doctor's office." He sat down on the beach, hard. "That was Amma and Meera."

Realization hit me. "That's how she caught it. It wasn't you."

Ajay shook his head, slowly. His eyes were wet. "It wasn't me."

I sat down next to him and put my hand on his shoulder.

He wiped at his face with both hands. "That's going to take a while to sink in."

"I bet."

Lethe stood before us, still smiling. But as the sun fully crested the horizon and its rays hit the island, she faded, mist in the morning sun.

"She's gone," Ajay said, looking around, as if she might be lurking behind us.

I nodded. "I don't think she'll be seen again."

My gaze caught the headland. The ruins of the house and the landslide had covered it in mud and brick. The tide surrounded it, waves dragging the looser rubble into the sea. I stood, and walked up to the edge, stepping into the foam that hissed up the sand. There was no question of going around it now, and no point in climbing over it. The cave was buried. I reached out to the wet rock.

"Charlotte," I said, almost to myself. "What do we do about Charlotte?"

I heard Ajay's soft step on the beach behind me and felt his hand, gentle on my shoulder.

"We're going to have to work out what to tell everyone about all this, so people will believe us. Other people will have known her, would have cared about her, about all of them: aunts or uncles, cousins or friends. We'll tell them where to find their bodies, if they can."

I nodded. Together we moved away from the headland and walked back along the beach. My shoes scuffed against the shingle. Out at sea, the white sails of small boats dotted the water between us and the mainland. I wondered if any of them were coming to the island, now that they remembered it.

Ajay stopped, and I paused next to him. There were tears in his eyes, but his face was alight as he turned to me. He smiled, then shook his head.

"It's you. It's really you. I found you."

Warmth rushed through me. He leaned in, as if he were about to kiss me. My heart leapt, but he hesitated.

"What is it?"

His gaze dropped to the ground. "You told me to leave you alone. I just want to make sure. I don't want to get in your face if you don't want me around."

My heart ached at his words, with love and regret, but I laughed, joy bubbling through me at this boy who cared so much about what I wanted.

"I don't want you to leave me alone. That is the absolute last thing I want."

His eyes flicked back up, and he grinned his wonderful grin. I put my arms around him and pulled him toward me. I felt the sun on my cheek as our lips met, felt the soft warmth of him, felt as if I were melting into him, like a perfect memory coming home.

When I was Oleander, I liked him way too much. When I was Charlotte, I fell for him all over again. Now I was both, and he was mine.

We kissed for a long time on the shore. When we finally broke apart, I leaned my head against his chest, against the soft fabric of his brown jumper. It was good to feel the warmth of his body so close to me, good to feel him breathe.

Soon, we'd have to try to get back to the mainland. Perhaps our parents were already on their way. I was in no hurry. I drank in the moment, savoring it, sealing it in my mind.

This memory was mine, and I would always keep it.

# ACKNOWLEDGEMENTS

Some of this book was written in the depths of the pandemic, squeezed into the cracks of life, while homeschooling small children and working full time around them. It was an escape from being just a mother and an employee, a reminder I had my own identity and imagination, and a source of sanity and stress. Thank you to my children for (sometimes!) letting me have a little time to myself to work on it.

The isolation made the feedback from family and friends more keenly appreciated than ever, especially as they were often going through their own tough times in those long months. Thank you so much to Helaine Becker, Bev Katz Rosenbaum, Lena Coakley, Leah Bobet, Jo Hope, Jill Belcher and Matt Blair. This book would literally not exist without you. I almost gave up on more than one occasion, and your kindness and enthusiasm stopped me from throwing this away in the bleakest days. Thank you too, to the Literary Consultancy for their feedback on an early draft.

Thank you to Barry Jowett, whose input is always wonderful and who put a huge amount of work into the restructuring of this book, Sarah Jensen for her work on the editing, including correcting all my Britishisms, Sarah Cooper for sorting out contract stuff and Luckshika Rajaratnam for following up on everything I kept forgetting to send.

Special thanks to the Canada Council for the Arts. It's impossible to say how much these grants mean to writers. Not only do they make writing possible, and lift the stress of making ends meet, but this one came at exactly the right time, and the encouragement it gave me added hugely to its value.

I'm so, so sorry if I forgot anyone, this book has been in progress for so many years that it's been hard to remember all the hands it has been through. I'm so glad it's finally done.

KATE BLAIR is a native of Hayling Island, UK, and is now a Canadian citizen living in Toronto. Her books for young readers have been nominated for such awards as the Manitoba Young Readers Choice Awards, the Saskatchewan Young Readers Choice Awards, and the Sunburst Awards. *Transferral* (2015) was starred selections of the Canadian Children's Book Centre's Best Books for Kids and Teens, and *Tangled Planet* (2017) received a starred review in *School Library Journal*. *The Magpie's Library* (2019) was a selection of the 2020 Forest of Reading Silver Birch Kids' Committee.

We acknowledge the sacred land on which Cormorant Books operates. It has been a site of human activity for 15,000 years. This land is the territory of the Huron-Wendat and Petun First Nations, the Seneca, and most recently, the Mississaugas of the Credit River. The territory was the subject of the Dish With One Spoon Wampum Belt Covenant, an agreement between the Iroquois Confederacy and Confederacy of the Ojibway and allied nations to peaceably share and steward the resources around the Great Lakes. Today, the meeting place of Toronto is still home to many Indigenous people from across Turtle Island. We are grateful to have the opportunity to work in the community, on this territory.

We are also mindful of broken covenants and the need to strive to make right with all our relations.